Uninvited Valor

The Forsaken Soldiers of WWII

*Based on the Epic True Story of the 442nd
Regimental Combat Team*

John C. Kiyonaga

Printed in the United States of America
Hardcover ISBN: 978-1-965253-19-9
Paperback ISBN: 978-1-965253-20-5
Ebook ISBN: 978-1-965253-21-2
Library of Congress Control Number: 2024945572

DartFrog Blue is the traditional publishing imprint of DartFrog Books, LLC.
301 S. McDowell St.
Suite 125-1625
Charlotte, NC 28204
www.DartFrogBooks.com

Continue the discussion online through our free book club www.DartFrogBooks.com/club

Dedicated to the Memory of

Joseph Yoshio Kiyonaga

1918 - 1977

1st Lieutenant (Infantry),
442nd Regimental Combat Team

THANK YOU

Thanks to Nan Catherine Kiyonaga, who rescued a lost battalion of one.

PROLOGUE

Orange County, Virginia
November 2023

"Dad, I'm joining the army."

I'd been daydreaming in my easy chair and my 23-year-old son had interrupted my evening Scotch. He answered the question on my face. "I miss being on a team."

He'd spent his college years rowing for a leading collegiate program, but the real reason hung behind him on the wall of our family room. Faded and creased, the framed photograph showed an unshaven man in filthy fatigues lighting another man's cigarette. The picture was taken in Northern Italy in 1944. It depicted my son's grandfather.

He had been one of thousands scorned by their fellow citizens—suspected, surveilled, and, in the case of some 127,000, even imprisoned by their own government, all for the sole fact of sharing the heritage of a nation that had struck the United States in a dastardly sneak attack.

These men didn't riot. They didn't sue. They didn't mount a public outcry deriding or demonizing their fellow citizens who had seconded their mistreatment. Instead, they volunteered by the thousands, many from the very camps where they had been wrongly confined, to serve those same citizens.

Most, but not all, of the characters that follow are fictitious. Their unit and its campaigns as depicted, however, are not. The 442nd Regimental Combat Team was a formation of the US Army that fought in the European Theater of the Second World War. Its soldiers lived their motto, "Go for Broke," and made their regiment the most highly decorated unit, to this day, in the Armed Services.

This is their story.

PART I

ISLAND BOY

NEVER THE SAME AGAIN

Wahiawa, Hawaii
December 7, 1941

Joe was tall for a Japanese. He shook himself out, settled his feet firmly into the turf, and addressed the ball in front of him. After a pause, he coiled his arms around himself before smoothly unwinding to bring the club head back towards the ball. Torquing his hips and shoulders, he felt the satisfying snap of contact as the ball rifled out over the fairway, tiny and white against the blue Hawaiian sky.

The rest of his foursome were murmuring their admiration and envy as he turned to face them and noticed a frenzy of tiny black dots off to the west, boiling against the sky between the peaks of the Kolekole Pass.

Joe picked up his bag and the four men began to walk down the fairway. He was the best golfer, perhaps because he was the tallest. All four men were Nisei, first-born Americans of parents who had emigrated to Hawaii from Japan. All four had studied together in high school and at the University of Hawaii.

"They must be the P-40s out of Hickam on a training flight," Sparky Masanobu said. Sparky was the only one who had gotten better grades than Joe. Shorter and quieter than the others, everyone tended to listen to what he said.

"On Sunday? *Haoles* don't work on Sundays, bruddah," Joe said, using the Hawaiian pidgin for white people.

Joe was likely to win the round and his friends would buy his lunch at the Halekulani, where the boys had reserved a table under the huge heliotrope tree on the hotel's terrace. Joe was excited to see Fumi, one of the girls that would be joining them. Fumi was one of the few girls to go "off island" for college. A prodigy from a family that was comparatively well fixed, she'd studied French at Barnard. Joe found her New York sophistication intriguing, probably because she laughed at his jokes.

Joe could not usually afford the Halekulani on his high school English teacher's salary, and he wanted *opihi* today. The small barnacles were notoriously expensive because the boys that picked them had to do so on the slippery rocks in the teeth of the ocean's waves. Joe liked them the way his mother served them— raw and chilled in a simple marinade of *shoyu,* soy sauce, with lime juice and garnished with *ogo,* seaweed.

He was imagining a dialogue that would charm Fumi when he noticed a far-off buzzing sound. The dots were now tiny airplane silhouettes, growing larger and louder.

"Why are they here?" Harry Masayoshi asked. "Their bombing range is off on the other side of the North Shore."

"Why are they so low?" asked Franny Fukuhara.

The four of them stopped walking.

The planes appeared to be flying directly at them, their buzz becoming a drone, becoming a roar. Suddenly, they were there—a thousand yards out and impossibly low—streaking over the adjacent sugarcane fields and closing the distance to the boys in an instant. No one said a word as the planes flashed overhead at fifty feet, but the red circles under the wings were unmistakable. The pilot of the last leaned out over his fuselage and looked directly down at them. He was Japanese.

No one spoke for a moment. Joe considered the imminent demise of his lunch plans and immediately felt ashamed.

The normally scholarly Sparky spoke first. "What the fuck?"

"Maybe they're some sort of special training mission made up to look like them?" said Franny. He was not normally the quickest on the uptake, but no one wanted to acknowledge the obvious.

Joe took a tentative step down the fairway toward his ball, but Sparky and Harry stood still while Franny took a half step after Joe.

"I don't think we're going to finish this round," Harry said, shaking his head.

They were on the ninth hole.

"Let's play through this hole to the half shack and listen to the radio there," Joe said.

This made sense. That was the nearest radio, and their car was not too far away. Something was definitely amiss, but no one was willing to accept that their island was actually under attack from a foreign power—particularly the one where their grandparents lived.

"Japan wouldn't attack us," ventured Franny. "We're not at war."

"How many Nisei know how to fly, Franny?" countered Sparky. "The only ones in the army are infantry, and they're only one battalion."

Joe was about to correct Sparky that the 100th Battalion was actually part of the National Guard when a sound like a huge steel door slamming at the end of a long corridor hit them like a body blow. As one, they turned toward the sound to see a geyser of black smoke erupting over the horizon from the direction of the navy base at Pearl Harbor. Balls forgotten, they started to run toward their car on the edge of the course.

At 8:00 on a Sunday morning, the road was nearly empty, and the car hit seventy on the way back to Honolulu. The boys said little. Each was consumed with his own questions and concerns. Joe's folks were on Molokai, but almost all his friends, including Fumi, lived in Honolulu. Had a bomb fallen prematurely on her civilian neighborhood? As the car drew closer, they could hear the attack over the Chevy's V-8 engine, an almost uninterrupted growl broken by sporadic explosions.

When they crested the last ridge in Mililani, Pearl Harbor and Honolulu beyond stretched out before them. Plumes of dense black smoke were everywhere, roiling out of the water in the harbor, the hangars at Ford Island, and even spots throughout the city. Planes careened above the harbor with smoky tracer rounds arcing lazily toward them from hundreds of points below. Boats—those that weren't burning—made wakes across the harbor. Sirens and staccato gunfire filled the ears and acrid smoke stung the nostrils and eyes. The planes seemed to be alone and wheeling almost leisurely in the sky while the scene beneath shuddered with chaos.

The boys were transfixed as the car drew steadily closer. Torpedoes lanced the water in rooster tails of spray as bombs detonated with a flash and the planes rolled and cut overhead with apparent impunity. Suddenly, a lone plane appeared from directly behind them, streaking straight into the maelstrom. They recognized the red and white shark's mouth prow of a Curtiss P-40 Warhawk, the workhorse pursuit plane of the Army Air Corps and avenger of the China skies of Chennault's Flying Tigers. The P-40 made straight for center mass of the attacking Japanese planes. As the boys watched, one of these started to trail black smoke and lose altitude. The P-40 continued unabated for several seconds until it, too, began to trail smoke. Joe found himself tearing up as the plane continued to descend and disappeared behind Diamond Head.

By now the boys were on the edge of Honolulu. No one was standing still. People ran this way and that. Cars sped by in all directions. A cacophony of machines, gunfire, and shouting roared in the background. As the car slowed for the traffic, Joe took in the houses around him on McCulley Street, just outside downtown. One of the houses had been hit. Its front had been blown out into the street and what remained was still burning.

A knot of people stood before a row of four oblong forms covered in blankets. The closest was small. A tiny hand clutching a *kokeshi* doll protruded from under the blanket.

The car had come to a stop now. Joe turned to his friends.

"Nothing will ever be the same again."

EXECUTIVE ORDER 9066

Someone had opened a window, but the cigarette smoke still hung over everyone in the room. As the president's closest advisor, Harry Hopkins had drawn the grandest conference room in the Old Executive Office Building across from the White House for his exclusive use. Hopkins now sat at the head of the table, lighting one cigarette with the butt of the last and casting his curiously bright eyes from one side of the room to the other. Gaunt almost to cadaverous, he held his listeners' attention as he spoke quietly.

"Uprooting and relocating every last one of them would be a mammoth undertaking," he said.

The Attorney General of California Earl Warren stirred in his seat to protest but stopped himself as Hopkins fixed him wordlessly with his eyes before continuing.

"Especially for them."

General George Marshall, Chief of Staff of the Army, nodded his head. "No question, Harry."

At this, Earl Warren broke in. "Would you disagree, General Marshall, that the entire West Coast, from the top of Washington to the bottom of California, is vulnerable to Japanese attack?"

The attorney general suggested the image of a Shakespearian-trained lumberjack. He would later reconstitute American race relations as the Chief Justice of the Supreme Court that outlawed segregation. This day, however, the former prosecutor was channeling the howls of his constituents, especially the California Chamber of Commerce, calling for the removal from California of all residents of Japanese descent.

If General Marshall was offended at the cross examination, he didn't show it. He responded evenly, "We are not in a position to fortify the entire coast, and never will be."

Earl Warren began to nod with satisfaction.

"But there is absolutely no indication the Japanese will ever be in a position to invade our Pacific Coast," Marshall continued.

Warren pounced. "Is that what you said before the Japs destroyed Pearl Harbor?"

Neither the general's expression nor his voice changed.

"Mr. Attorney General, there's no comparison between a two-hour air strike and an invasion across the entire Pacific with the logistical support that would entail."

Harry Hopkins looked around the room. Aides to each of the attendees sat along the walls. Two graying FBI agents sat without expression directly behind their boss, J. Edgar Hoover, who sat opposite him.

"Edgar," Hopkins said, "you're in the best position to know. Are the Japanese Americans a threat?"

The FBI director was a diminutive man with wide-set eyes that took up too much of his face. He pushed his hands across the table in front of him.

"Harry, my people have queried local law enforcement across the entire West Coast. No one reports any suspicious activity—nor, in fact, any reason at all to suspect disloyalty among the Japanese there."

Earl Warren didn't give Harry Hopkins time to respond.

"Of course, the Japs didn't advertise their intention to sneak attack our boys at Pearl Harbor, either," he sneered.

Hoover was unfazed.

"That's not entirely true, General," Hoover said. "They'd cabled their embassy to sever diplomatic relations the day before, but the cable was misplaced."

Earl Warren had missed World War I after being rejected from officer training for hemorrhoids. Harry Hopkins' secretary, Philip Royster, thought he saw a slight smile cross General Marshall's face when Hoover addressed the California politician with military rank.

Royster was a 25-year-old graduate of the University of Pennsylvania from Roystertown, Pennsylvania. His mother and Harry Hopkins had been friends since working together for the New York City Bureau of Child Welfare earlier in the century. Phil's father thought he needed "a little seasoning" before joining the family investment bank in Philadelphia, so Phil had followed his father into the First Troop—a Pennsylvania National Guard unit dating back to the Revolution with its own stable of hunters and polo ponies—and signed on to public service at the feet of the president's closest adviser.

Phil sat now behind his boss, taking in the fencing across the table. He knew his boss did not particularly like Hoover; in fact, Hopkins suspected Hoover of being attracted to other men. The FBI director shared a suite at the Shoreham Hotel with his patrician second in command, Clyde Tolson, and the two had a dedicated lunch table at Columbia Country Club just outside Washington in suburban Maryland. But Hoover's apparently unerring success at gang-busting had subsumed any questions about his personal life.

The attorney general of California was not finished. His words rolled orotund down his nose at his audience.

"The people of California, the people of this nation, cannot live with a snake slithering freely in their midst."

Harry Hopkins restored order. "General Marshall, where is the army on this?"

The general spoke as if he were describing the stocking of a fuel depot.

"Harry, the army has identified no pressing threat from the coastal Japanese, but I—we—serve at the pleasure of the president."

Warren smiled thinly. "Of course, internal security is not the army's bailiwick, is it?" he said.

"Of course not," Hoover interjected. "It's the Federal Bureau of Investigation's."

He paused for a moment before continuing.

"If we expel the West Coast Japanese, it will not be for reasons of security."

Harry Hopkins slapped the arms of his chair lightly and stood. "Thank you, gentlemen."

As the others gathered themselves to leave, Phil helped his boss into his overcoat against the damp February air of the former swamp that was official Washington. The charcoal herringbone was as heavy as a horse blanket and enveloped Hopkins, leaving his gaunt head perched like a lollipop on his impossibly narrow neck. Hopkins nodded his thanks and exhaled smoke as he spoke.

"The president expects me in the Oval Office. Come along."

Phil recognized a signal change in his fortunes. He had never before met the president. Suddenly, he regretted wearing the stylish striped shirt with his First Troop tie instead of the bright white shirt his father favored. His boss paused just before leaving the building to light another cigarette from the ember of the one in his mouth.

The wind on 17th Street went right through Phil's overcoat, but Hopkins seemed not to notice, spilling ashes across the front of his coat as he buried his hands in his hip pockets and expelled streams of dense white smoke into the icy air.

After the doorman had taken their coats, Phil was more than a little concerned when his boss sailed into the Oval Office without discarding his cigarette—until he saw the man waiting for them behind the Endurance desk with an ebony holder and smoldering cigarette held firmly between his teeth.

Phil's family were not fans of the president. They regarded the New Deal as a threat to the social order. Phil's father's denunciations were forgotten, however, the instant the president's eyes set on Phil and his face lit up in a smile. He leaned forward in his chair to extend his hand.

"You must be the bright young Phil that Harry's been bragging about."

Phil's first commander had spoken to the men about the importance of inspiring personal loyalty, and for the first time, Phil realized what he meant. As the president beamed at him, Phil felt like he was back in the Cub Scouts, his father gripping his shoulders and congratulating him for coming in first on the obstacle course. At seven, the warmth in his chest had filled his entire being as he'd looked up at his father smiling down at him. Now, despite the war on, Phil honestly felt as if the man seated before him cared about nothing in the world more than meeting him.

Phil couldn't speak, so he just shook the president's hand. After a moment, he let go and the president motioned him into a chair.

"Join us please, Phil."

Phil still couldn't breathe as he took his seat. His boss smiled quietly as he settled into his own chair.

The president did the same, raising his voice to say, "Alonzo, the provisions, if you don't mind."

At this, he turned to Harry, the smile leaving his face. "These West Coast Japanese are a sticky wicket, eh?"

Perhaps because he was crippled by polio, the president was fond of sports analogies.

Harry Hopkins nodded unhappily. "The Army is indifferent," he said, "and FBI sees no threat at all."

The president started to raise his eyebrows in happy surprise before Phil's boss continued.

"California is implacable, though."

At this moment, the president's butler, Alonzo Fields, came into the room with a rolling bar cart. Tall, black, and wearing a bright white jacket and gloves, the butler bore through the room like a sloop on a gentle wind—a war chief greeting his guests. The president, who had grown up sailing on Oyster Bay, smiled. "The sun's over the yardarm."

He turned to the cart the butler had left next to his wheelchair. Three frosted Martini glasses stood on a silver platter next to a bucket of ice, a silver cocktail shaker, and frosted bottles of Beefeater gin and Noilly Prat vermouth. Without a word, the president used his hand to drop ice into the shaker and then filled it nearly to the top with the frigid gin. He filled the cap of the Noilly Prat bottle with vermouth and added this to the mix.

He didn't touch the shaker. Instead, he turned to the plate of garnishes and asked Phil, "Will an olive suit, Phil?"

Phil had finally found his voice. "Yes, Mr. President."

The president speared three olives on toothpicks and dropped each one into a glass. He took the crystal cocktail stirrer and turned it once, slowly, in the shaker and poured the contents into each glass. Alonzo Fields placed one glass before the president and then gave one to Phil and one to his boss. The crystal neck of Phil's glass was numbingly cold and the chandelier lights played off the surface of the drink.

Phil was savoring the sharp scent of the gin when the president spoke.

"What are we drinking to, men?"

Phil looked up to see both men looking at him. Without thinking, he stood, grateful for not spilling his drink, and held out his glass.

He was still searching for words when he heard himself say, "To my Commander in Chief."

Phil took his first sip while still on his feet. Suddenly, his customary beer was insufficient. The icy gin cleansed and filled his whole head. As he resumed his seat, Phil saw the president lean back in his chair, close his eyes, and take a long pull on his creation. Replacing his glass on his desk, he removed his cigarette from its holder and inserted a new one. Phil noticed a gold ring before the filter and surmised the cigarette had been made for the president. Before realizing it, he was back on his feet extending his lighter.

The president accepted the light and smiled. "No dope, this one, Harry."

The president alternated between his drink and his smoke in silence until each was half gone. Then he turned to Harry Hopkins again.

"You know, Harry, I'm sensitive to mistreating Orientals. My grandfather Warren made the Delano fortune shipping opium from Turkey to the Chinese on his sailing clippers."

"There's nothing for it, Mr. President," Harry Hopkins responded. "Warren is out for their blood. We leave the California Japanese in place and the entire state will fester against you."

"No other state will take them—not at liberty anyway," the president said thoughtfully.

Harry Hopkins nodded. "The Governor of Idaho promises a 'Jap hanging from every pine tree' if they're released into his state."

Were he not dizzy with regard for him, Phil would have heard the colliding beads of the anthracite abacus that was his president's political compass.

The president finished his martini and shook his head sadly.

"California is too important," he said. "Prepare an executive order relocating the West Coast Japanese to internment camps in the interior."

Harry Hopkins had prepared.

"The exclusion order has already been drafted," Hopkins replied. "I'll have Ickes select sites for the construction of the camps."

The president said nothing.

"I'll bring Executive Order 9066 by for your signature within the week," Hopkins said.

GOONS

Honolulu, Hawaii
6 Months After Pearl Harbor

Joe's small apartment on McCully Street was cool in the midday heat. A half pound of raw tuna trucked in that morning from the Aloha Pier waited in the ice box with two chilled pre-embargo Sapporo beers. He needed to finish grading two more sophomore English papers before his light lunch and an afternoon of golf with Sparky and the guys.

The knock at the front door startled him.

Joe opened the door to two men. They were standing in the covered walkway that connected the second story apartments, both wearing dark suits instead of the khaki or cream linen favored by professional men from the islands. The closest man was heavyset with oiled dark hair and a neck that overflowed his shirt and tie—Hardy of *Laurel and Hardy*— but without the smile. The only thing Joe noticed about the second man was his too-large Adam's apple perched uncomfortably on a too-thin neck like Ichabod Crane's.

Neither Hardy nor Ichabod spoke before walking past Joe into the foyer.

"Smells like bad fish in here," the first man said.

Ichabod was looking at the trash basket in the foyer.

"You too good for Pabst?" he asked, pulling a Sapporo empty from the bin.

Joe's heart was racing. He asked, although he already knew the answer, "Who are you?"

Joe had done nothing wrong, but the federal government had already rounded up hundreds of older male Issei, Japanese immigrants, and sent them to a converted warehouse on Sand Island. Joe's old Kendo teacher, Ogata-san, had been taken to the barbed wire enclosure, and so, too, had the octogenarian Buddhist priest from his home island of Molokai.

Still, Hawaii's ethnic Japanese had it better than their mainland counterparts. Entire families on the West Coast had been given seventy-two hours to abandon their homes, schools, and businesses and report for "relocation" to internment camps. Over 100,000 people would eventually be consigned to these windblown pest holes across the country.

Joe knew they weren't taking Nisei from Hawaii—there were too damned many of them. Still, his chest constricted.

Hardy narrowed his eyes and widened his smile in response to Joe's question. Ichabod just loomed impassively.

Joe held their stare for another moment but could not withstand their silence.

"You've interrupted my work," he said in a tone of affronted innocence.

"What do you do?" Hardy asked. "Shovel shit?"

Joe took pride in his job. Few boys out of the plantation towns made it to college, much less into the teaching profession.

"I'm an English teacher. Have you come here for help?"

Hardy's backhand exploded across his right cheek.

"Shut the fuck up, Jap. You'll speak when you're spoken to."

Joe could smell the man's breath.

Stunned or not, Joe's fists balled involuntarily, but he saw the beginnings of a smile on Ichabod's face and willed himself to remain still. At 6'4", Joe was much taller than either of the men, but he knew that FBI agents always carried sidearms.

The three of them stood in silence for several seconds before Hardy spoke again.

"We know you're listening to Jap radio broadcasts."

Joe said nothing. He'd always listened to them, if only to keep up his Japanese, but now he was also curious about the Japanese take on the war. Several steel hulks dead in the water at Pearl Harbor were hard to ignore, especially when one had over a thousand sailors still inside. Japan's recent seizure of Corregidor in Manila Bay hadn't reassured anyone, either.

Hardy crossed into the main room and helped himself to the sofa made of monkey pod wood. His bulk all but obliterated the bright blue and yellow pandanus pattern of the cushions. Ichabod followed Hardy but remained standing. Neither had identified himself.

"Why the fuck do you care what Tojo and the rest of the cocksucking Japs have to say?" Hardy asked.

Speaking of sex, Joe was tempted to ask whether Hardy had ever managed to get a woman to overlook his appearance. But he did notice that Hardy was at least now referring to the "Japs" in the third person.

"Why is it so important to you? Who are you talking to?" Hardy pressed.

Joe realized his heart rate had fallen. Getting slapped had actually calmed him somewhat, and he was beginning to wonder if these two were blindly fishing. If they'd thought he was plotting with someone, which he wasn't, they would have spoken the person's name.

The Chief of Naval Operations had conveniently blamed Pearl Harbor on a "Fifth Column" of ethnic Japanese in the islands. The haole press had taken up the cry, but it wasn't the ethnic Japanese who had left the American fighter planes at Hickam and Bellows conveniently arrayed in neat rows, ready for the marauding Zeroes to stitch them up with their machine guns. Prior to the Pearl Harbor attack, General Short had ordered that all Army Air Corps planes be parked mid-field specifically to avoid sabotage from this supposed Fifth Column.

"You think we don't know?" Hardy continued, his voice higher than he probably wanted.

Joe continued to look evenly at the men. He was beginning to see that these two, or at least Hardy, would just keep talking if he said nothing.

"The whole building can hear you listening to that jibber jabber late at night," Hardy added.

With this, Joe realized why they were there. Two attractive young women from the mainland had moved into the apartment next to him a month ago, part of a growing swell of military and civilians flooding the islands to prepare the push out into the Pacific. He guessed they wouldn't be joining him for drinks anytime soon.

Joe still said nothing. He had read somewhere that the definition of stupid is to persist in something already demonstrated not to work.

Hardy obviously hadn't read this. He hoisted himself from the sofa and crossed to the ice box. Beyond a breakfast table and two chairs, all made of monkey pod, there was little else in the room.

Hardy's eyes widened as he retrieved the tuna, neatly wrapped in wax paper. Slowly, he unwrapped Joe's meal, which was worth half a day of Joe's wages. His face fell as he realized what it was, and he threw it to the floor.

"This shit makes your skin yellow."

Joe decided he would rinse it off and eat it anyway.

Hardy and Ichabod exchanged glances. No one spoke. Joe was trying to remember whether any rule forbade listening to Japanese broadcasts when Hardy spoke again.

"The Bureau is responsible for security in these islands."

Joe still said nothing. Instead, he just stood there, gangly in a red and white aloha shirt and horn-rimmed glasses. After a moment, he shifted his weight from one foot to the other.

"There's only one reason for refusing to cooperate," Hardy said, his voice a little quieter.

"We're not here to hear ourselves talk," Ichabod said, trying to recapture the momentum with an edge of menace. The bobbing Adam's apple ruined the effect.

Joe was now convinced that these two had nothing at all beyond bluster. He slowly looked from one to the other as Hardy and Ichabod exchanged glances again. Joe took a seat at his breakfast table and crossed his legs languidly, fixing them with an impassive look.

"We already know who's helping the Japs," Hardy said, moving to stand over Joe. "We're giving you a chance to help yourself."

Joe couldn't be sure, but he thought he remembered this ploy from a desperate spy in a Charlie Chan movie.

"If you knew, you wouldn't be asking questions," he said.

"Don't tell us our business, Jap," Ichabod snapped. He was about to continue, but stopped awkwardly when he caught Hardy's look.

"The truth is"—Hardy sounded almost apologetic—"we could always use help… and you could always use ours."

Joe had trouble surmising the sort of help these two would provide after slapping him around. They were with the same government that was rounding up his people all over the West Coast. He was about to explain that no one was helping anyone he knew when Ichabod tried to regain the upper hand.

"You're not even supposed to be here."

That was enough. Joe was proud of his English—crisp, clean, and the reason he'd been hired to teach it. But he reverted to pidgin to tell the agents they were confused.

"I was born here. You broke da brain."

Hardy became plaintive.

"The Bureau understands that people stick with their own kind," he said.

Joe just did not have any more time for them. He was remembering the tiny hand clutching the kokeshi doll. He could feel his pulse in his ears as his words came out in a low growl.

"If they were our own kind, then why did they bomb us, goddammit?"

WHITE SENSEI

"Joe, I'm so glad you were able to meet me."

Roger Alton had taken the steamer from Maui and invited Joe to dinner. Mr. Alton had been Joe's headmaster at Lahainaluna, a scholarship boys' boarding school on Maui that was the oldest high school west of the Rockies. Founded by Protestant missionaries in 1831 as Lahainaluna Seminary, the school boarded and educated island boys tuition-free in exchange for labor. Joe had never owned a pair of shoes when he arrived at the school from Molokai in the eighth grade. He earned his keep cutting sugarcane and breaking rocks in a quarry.

Joe still remembered the first time he'd set eyes on his headmaster. He'd been tired, dirty, and not a little seasick after the rough crossing from Molokai. Staggering onto the wharf from the ferry, Joe beheld an immaculately dressed man standing lean and straight next to a spotless gray Packard Saloon. Mr. Alton wore an ivory linen suit just like Dr. Goodhue, an East Coast Brahmin, reputed to be first cousin to Calvin Coolidge, who lived on Molokai and tended the lepers at Kalaupapa Leprosarium and everyone else on the island. Joe had never actually spoken to the doctor, but he remembered him driving into Kaunakakai in a beautiful car—a Rolls Royce, he would later learn—to care for people. Once Joe had seen him standing next to the car on the road up to the Pali with a brace of pheasant in one hand and an open double gun in the other. He looked like everything Joe would like to become and Joe had decided that Roger Alton would show him the way.

Although Lahainaluna was no longer run by the American Board of Commissioners of Foreign Missions, the school's Protestant roots still informed its choices. Roger Alton had grown up in Beacon Hill and graduated from the Hill School and Harvard. Armed with a bachelor's in classics and a varsity letter in rowing, he had decamped for Hawaii and Lahainaluna with his young wife Araminta after being interviewed by an elder of the Pilgrim Trinitarian Congregational Church. Mr. Alton taught Joe how to speak and how to dress and bought him his first pair of shoes—brown Alden Bluchers that were expensive but indestructible and big enough to survive a growth spurt. Mrs. Alton taught Joe how to dance and to set a table for company. By eighteen, Joe had become a Boston Brahmin— Molokai Model. He had also won the American Legion College Scholarship for the entire territory.

Now Joe sat with his mentor at a small waterfront place waiting for their dinner. Roger Alton had trouble meeting his former student's eyes.

"Joe, I can't tell you how disappointed I am. Ashamed, really."

Joe nodded gently.

"We're a nation founded on Christian values, but we've locked up an entire race even though no one has been found to be disloyal," Mr. Alton continued.

By this time, some 120,000 ethnic Japanese from the West Coast, and a few Hawaii elders, had been permanently consigned to internment camps. These were encircled with barbed wire and guard towers and were usually to be found in desert or other worthless real estate. Entire families were crammed into hasty tar paper shacks with internal curtains suspended for privacy. They had left everything behind—homes and businesses—to be sold for a fraction of their value if no friendly soul could be found to help. One old man, beside himself, had scaled the perimeter wire, only to be shot dead by guards in front of his fellow internees.

Still, there had been little outcry about the camps beyond the objections raised by the churches, the Protestant missionary community in particular.

"It's a triumph of ignorance, Joe," his educator continued. "To target an entire people simply because of their ancestry hearkens back to the Civil War, our nation's greatest test and the signal triumph of its founding principles."

Joe didn't disagree, so he simply kept nodding. He hadn't seen his old teacher in seven years, but they had corresponded, the teacher always curious about his student's progress through life. Out of respect for his mentor, Joe had worn a blazer and foulard tie to dinner instead of an aloha shirt. Mr. Alton had worn one of his apparently innumerable linen suits and a bow tie that Joe had come to recognize as that of his college club, the Porcellian.

Mr. Alton had told him about Harvard's oldest club, which he called "The Pork," at Joe's first meal at Lahainaluna. Joe had been fixated on the tiny pigs' heads that festooned his headmaster's tie.

"Ah," Mr. Alton had said. "My college club, the Porcellian. We eat roast pork every Friday evening."

Mr. Alton's appearance had not changed much since their first meeting - a few more lines on the face, but the same quiet eyes and erect carriage. He'd joined the new boys at their table in the dining room their first night at school.

He'd tried to draw each boy out, but Joe had been a challenge. He'd spent far more time reading than talking until then.

"What do you enjoy doing on Molokai, Joe?" Mr. Alton had asked.

Joe was happy for an excuse to put down the unfamiliar silverware.

"I like to hunt," he'd answered.

"I understand you have superb pheasant shooting in the uplands."

"Francolin and quail, too," Joe responded brightly, then added reflexively, "sir."

"What do you use, Joe?" Mr. Alton had continued. "Do you have a dog?"

Mr. Alton was probably accustomed to majestic pointers, long and imperial in their bearing, but Joe was a subsistence hunter. His companion was Kiichi, a one-eyed *poi* dog, a wandering mutt that had followed him home off the mountain one day. Short of leg and thick of body, Kiichi was the color of a wharf rat. Joe and his parents surmised that the dog had lost his eye to a cruel owner and had decided to follow Joe home.

Kiichi's technique was not to scent the wind or quarter a field like his European counterparts. He simply walked next to Joe until he somehow sensed the proximity of a hidden bird. Rather than lock into a commanding point, he would run at it headlong, leaving Joe a split second to shoulder his shotgun before the bird got up and flew out of range. Kiichi never failed to bring back the birds Joe hit.

"I use my dog, Kiichi," Joe answered.

"My mother raised German Pointers at our place in the Berkshire Mountains." Alton smiled. "What breed is Kiichi?"

Mr. Alton probably realized too late that Kiichi was most likely an accidental affront to considered procreation, but twelve-year-old Joe had rescued this kind adult by creating a breed exclusively to comprise his best friend.

"Molokai Mastiff, bred for loyalty and intelligence," he replied without pause.

Now, the two men sat facing each other as the waiter brought two beers. Mr. Alton raised his glass.

"To friends."

"To friends, Mr. Alton," Joe replied.

"Joe," Mr. Alton continued, "you must know some of the people militating for the formation of a Nisei Army unit."

"I know a number of them. Harry Masayoshi from my class is one of them," Joe said. "I'm not sure I'm with them though," he continued, anticipating the next question.

Mr. Alton nodded. "There's a young man on the mainland who's in jail for refusing to report for relocation. Brave, actually," he said.

Joe had read about Fred Korematsu. "Principled certainly, but..." Joe stopped.

"There's no right or wrong answer, Joe," Mr. Alton helped him. "You didn't create the problem and it's very complicated."

"1 was hoping you would tell me what I should do," Joe answered.

"1 can't," answered his teacher. "I really just came out to show you that I'm sorry that you've been forced into a choice and that I'll respect whatever choice you make."

Their steaks arrived. Both were charred on the outside and barely pink in the middle—"Pittsburghed"—but Joe was having trouble attacking one of his favorite meals. He was remembering the sting of Agent Hardy's backhand.

"I'm not sure I see the point in serving a country that treats my people like garbage," he said.

Mr. Alton just nodded.

"It's like congratulating someone who cheats you at golf," Joe added.

Mr. Alton knew what Joe was talking about.

Joe had arrived at Lahainaluna a voracious reader, and Mr. Alton had broadened his fare from Zane Gray and Kipling to Cooper, Crane, Steinbeck and, eventually, Fitzgerald and Hemingway. But aside from reading constantly, Joe had found little to occupy his time at Lahainaluna. He was too frail for football, too awkward for basketball, and altogether too slow for baseball. On impulse, Mr. Alton had invited him to tag along with two other boys for a round of golf at the course built for the managers of the Haleakala Ranch.

"Try to relax while you concentrate," Mr. Alton had told Joe when he addressed his first ball. It had become immediately apparent that Joe could do just that. Free of a ridiculing audience, he had shown himself able to choreograph his entire body into a very coherent swing. Mr. Alton had decided on the third hole to create a Lahainaluna Golf Team.

The team's banner match that year was hosted by the Punahou School in Honolulu, a school established to educate planters' sons who didn't want to go back East to places like Groton or the Hill School. Its golfers had been playing on private courses before becoming teenagers.

Lahainaluna had dispatched its four best players, led by Joe, to meet the challenge.

Punahou's course had never seen melanin-rich people, beyond the grounds staff. Joe and his friends had stormed the course, emerging as the front runners by the 10th hole. The

Punahou team had responded by cheating—furtively moving balls, replacing them, and doctoring score cards. Worse, they were almost gleefully obvious about it, and their captain sneered at the Lahainaluna golfers throughout the match.

Joe had been determined to lodge a complaint—until he'd spotted the Punahou captain's parents at the 18th hole. Beyond a set scowl, the father was featureless. The mother, however, was the image of her son and she was radiant. As the Punahou team finished, she clutched her husband's arm and gazed adoringly at the cheater. After seeing her, Joe just hadn't been able to complain. Lahainaluna had lost the match.

What he remembered most, however, was Mr. Alton. He had walked the course during the play and had seen the cheating. He stood off to one side as a subdued Lahainaluna team had congratulated their opponents. Then he'd shaken Joe's hand, holding his eyes in silence.

Now Joe shook his head. "The stakes now are a little bigger than a golf trophy."

"Ofcourse," Mr. Alton agreed. "But a fine gesture is no less fine just because it happens to benefit someone who is undeserving. You didn't do what you did for the Punahou captain."

"I wish I hadn't done it," Joe muttered.

"No, you don't," responded his teacher. "The point is that you didn't do it for him, just like Harry and the others aren't talking about joining the army for President Roosevelt or General Dewitt."

General Dewitt, the man who had issued and enforced the relocation order, was not liked by most Japanese Americans.

"The order is an abomination," Mr. Alton continued. "The state's power to take your liberty is its greatest - to be exercised only with due process. The right to defend against an accusation goes back to the Magna Carta, but the internees haven't even been accused, much less given any sort of trial."

Joe nodded.

Mr. Alton shook his head. "I don't have your answer, Joe, because I just don't know, but your decision may be the most important of your life."

Joe started to nod before his teacher finished.

"Just don't make it based on your feelings for a president who got turned away by The Pork."

SPARKY

Honolulu, Hawaii
11 Months After Pearl Harbor

Sparky had been Joe's best friend at Lahainaluna and at the University of Hawaii. He'd grown up in Hilo and, like Joe, he'd assuaged the solitude of his childhood with reading.

Even though Joe was eight inches taller, the boys had become inseparable. Sparky had even become the most motivated and least gifted member of Lahainaluna's golf team.

Sparky was a natural scholar; he just loved to learn new things. Joe had been less driven, loathe to immerse himself in any area that did not appeal. The boys had competed for valedictorian, but Sparky had narrowly beaten Joe's grades. However, he had lost the American Legion Scholarship to Joe, whose selection as captain of the golf team had sealed that award for him.

Now the two young men sat at a Hotel Street noodle emporium where Joe had invited Sparky to celebrate the latter's recent acceptance to Harvard Law School. They'd both ordered *udon* buckwheat noodles with braised yellowtail tuna jaw, *hamachi,* and were drinking icy beer as the soup was prepared.

"I need to talk to you," Sparky said.

Joe could barely hear him over the other patrons in the crowded restaurant. Always earnest, Sparky's air was worryingly serious.

"I'm listening, brah," Joe said before drinking more of his beer.

Sparky leaned in with a pained expression. "I've done something I'm ashamed of."

Joe could not imagine his preternaturally responsible friend doing anything that would give him the least pause, but he felt flattered that Sparky would come to him for counsel.

"I'm sure you're overreacting," Joe said.

"I'm not. You're the only one I can talk to." Sparky lifted his eyes to Joe. "You wouldn't understand because you've always had Fumi."

Pretty and unselfconscious, Fumi was much admired, but Joe had never "had" her. In fact, he'd stopped speaking to her weeks earlier when he'd decided she'd become too receptive to some guy from Punahou who'd played tennis for Columbia. He was pleased, however, that Sparky apparently credited Joe's air of sophistication with the fair sex. He decided that Sparky needed some of his steel.

"Women are like buses," Joe said. "There's always another one."

Sparky just shook his head. "I'm serious, Joe. I've really disappointed myself."

Joe understood another male's need for his experience. He set his beer aside. "What the hell have you done?"

Sparky was actually squirming in his chair.

"It's just that I've been with a girl that really challenges my image of myself, my self-respect," he whispered.

Joe himself had not been entirely unfamiliar with women whose appearance might have given his friends pause. None, however, had left him so reduced as he now found his best friend. He leaned back and cast his eyes at the ceiling, moving his hands expansively over the table. "Brah, we're men. We're supposed to take what we need."

"No. You don't get it, Joe. This girl is beyond not pretty..."

"Cut it out, Sparky," Joe said, wondering what she looked like. "We've all been there," he intoned with as much sympathy as his voice could muster.

"No, you really don't get it, Joe. This goes beyond a forgivable lapse in standards."

Joe was trying to imagine the poor girl. He continued his charity, reaching over and grabbing his friend's forearm. "Get a hold of yourself. I'm sure you're exaggerating."

"I'm not."

"We've all been there, Sparky," Joe said, thanking God that he hadn't.

Sparky kept shaking his head miserably.

"Not true, Joe."

Joe drew himself up in his chair and reached over to take Sparky by his shoulders.

"Sparky, please take a moment to put this in perspective."

Joe was positively magisterial now, quietly gifting his friend the strength he lacked. Sparky lowered his eyes to the table again.

"I have, Joe. It's just that you wouldn't say that if you'd seen Shizuko..."

Joe stiffened and released his friend's shoulders. "What did you say her name was?"

THE BOYS

Honolulu, Hawaii
13 Months After Pearl Harbor

"Guys, you're the first to know. I've asked Hibiki to marry me. I haven't even told Mom."

They had circled four chairs around a footlocker in Franny's spartan room at the YMCA. Franny had chosen one of the boys' periodic poker games to share his news but had been too excited to wait until the cards had been dealt or the beers had been opened.

"Don't sweat it, Franny," Joe quickly interjected. "The next one is sure to say 'Yes.'"

Franny was undeterred.

"You're all invited."

"What do you mean, we're invited?" Joe continued. "No one else would come."

None of the boys was surprised. Franny and Hibiki had been inseparable since Franny's mother had introduced them a year earlier – an assisted, if not an arranged, courtship.

"That's great, Franny," said Harry, standing and extending his hand to Franny. "We'll see less of you, but she's a great girl."

Hibiki was from Waimanalo where her father worked cattle for the Gunstock Ranch. Her mother knew Franny's widowed mother from church. Franny's father had worked for Dillingham and had died in a dredging accident when Franny was twelve. The oldest of four children, Franny had helped raise his younger siblings after his father's death.

"Honestly, Franny, I couldn't see you marrying anyone else." Sparky smiled as he stood, too. "We all think she's great."

Franny relaxed visibly. "We plan to raise a brood of mathematicians," he said, laughing.

Franny had famously "discovered" that the Pythagorean Theorem was flawed while the boys were in the third form at school. The truth was, he had skipped a digit in his calculations, but he didn't realize it before telling everyone that he had disproven the most fundamental rule of mathematics. Incriminatory figures in hand, he had announced his discovery to the morning assembly. The geometry teacher, Mr. Callahan, had let him down gently. Franny had taken the ensuing ridicule lightly.

"Should we get married now or wait?" asked Franny.

"Why wait, unless you're not sure?" Joe replied.

"I'm sure, dammit, but it looks like we might be able to join the army."

At this, the room fell silent. Ever since Pearl Harbor, all military age Nisei had been reclassified by the Draft Board as 4F, ineligible for service. The only exception had been the 100th Battalion, the Nisei Infantry formation of the Hawaii National Guard. Already constituted and trained when the Japanese attacked, it had been allowed to remain in existence and was now deployed to Southern Italy. Only months into its engagement, the 100th was developing a reputation for accomplishing what other units could not.

Younger Nisei were initially divided. Many sought to serve as the 100th was doing. Others, like Joe and many of the Nisei in the camps, were ambivalent. They felt betrayed, or at least abandoned, by their own country.

"Why the hell should we join the army, Franny?" Joe shot at him. "The government is locking our people up all over the mainland and not a single one of us has shown any disloyalty to our country."

"They must have a reason," Franny said uncertainly.

"You're right, Franny," Joe snarled. "They do have a reason. We look different."

"Cut it out, Joe. You're playing into their hands," Harry said.

Harry had an almost unconscious assurance, born probably of his almost insuperable athletic gifts. He could move any kind of ball like he'd been born to do nothing else. Baseball, basketball, football—he'd lettered in all of them throughout high school and college. He was even reputed to have a cousin playing shortstop for Nagoya.

Harry leaned toward Joe over the cards. "Get mad and you're only proving them right."

After Pearl Harbor, the Hearst Press on the mainland had maintained a steady screed of suspicion and scorn against the Japanese Americans. Countless white Californians had walked off with Issei truck farms and businesses after their owners had been forced to relocate to the camps.

"We're called foreign and sneaky," Harry continued. "It's up to us to prove them wrong."

"Why should we care what they think, Harry?" Joe was getting heated. "They obviously don't care about being fair."

"Who exactly is 'they,' Joe?" Harry was getting heated himself. "Since when have we disliked haoles?"

As a star athlete, Harry had made close friends of his white teammates, most of whom were already serving in the military. But all the boys had haole friends, lots of them. Harry had just reminded Joe of Mr. Alton and all the teachers who had helped him along.

"What's your favorite game?" Harry pressed.

Joe started to protest the question's relevance, but Harry cut him off.

"It's baseball, right? Or it would be if you could play worth a shit. And who's your favorite actress? It's Rita Hayworth. And your favorite band?"

Joe shrugged his shoulders.

"It's Dorsey, Joe. My point is, we're all more haole than you seem to think."

Sparky had regained his usual aplomb since his last meeting with Joe. He placed a hand on a shoulder of each belligerent.

"We all have haole friends," he said, "but the vast majority of haoles have never laid eyes on one of us."

No one disagreed—no one ever did with Sparky—so he continued.

"Most haoles only know we look like the enemy; an enemy they're not sure we'll beat."

Joe himself had initially harbored unspoken doubts, particularly after the Japanese had rolled up the Philippines and Singapore. But the sheer scale of Pearl Harbor's transformation from smoking ruin to humming hub of the Pacific Fleet in a matter of weeks had impressed him with America's material and managerial might.

Sparky shrugged his shoulders.

"Consider our choices, guys. We know what the Nazis have done. They've butchered half of Europe."

No one could disagree.

"The Japanese are just as bad, maybe worse," Sparky continued. "Look what they did in Nanking."

The Rape of Nanking had horrified the world five years earlier. The photographs of innumerable piled bodies—many of them naked—were indelible.

"Just imagine what they'd do here," Harry cut in. "Picture for a second Waikiki with a thousand armed *Eta* descending on the sunbathing *wahini* girls."

Japan still had a caste system, although it was less conspicuous than India's. The "Eta" were comparable to India's "Untouchables," occupying the lowest rung of the social ladder. They collected "night soil," sewage.

"We don't need to imagine anything," Sparky growled. "The murdering sons of bitches came here and killed 2,000 guys sitting down to their Sunday pancakes. The 100th is already losing guys," he continued. "Everyone is." He looked around at his friends. "How is this not our fight, too?"

OPPORTUNITY

The First Lady did not invite familiarity.

Phil was flattered to be at table with the First Couple, his boss Harry Hopkins, and the president's indispensable personal assistant, Missy LeHand. Mrs. Roosevelt sat opposite her husband with their guests ranged between them.

"Harry, you're working too hard. You're skin and bones," she'd said by way of greeting Hopkins.

Phil she had acknowledged languidly. "Welcome, young man."

Missy she had acknowledged with a nod.

The president's attention was consumed with the bottle proffered by his butler. "Alonzo, what is this?"

"Chateauneuf du Pape, Mr. President."

Alonzo drew back the linen wrapping to show the president the label and raised escutcheon of the vineyard.

"The Chef selected it for the lamb chops," he said.

"Please tell me they're not overcooked?"

"No, sir. I checked myself. They're pink and perfect on the inside, sir."

"Wonderful. Now let's check this wine."

The president held the wine under his nose and inhaled more elaborately than necessary as his eyes travelled the table to register his guests' entertainment. His wife appeared not to notice. He swirled the contents before pouring some into his mouth and ruminating fiercely with his eyes closed.

"Bully bottle," he exclaimed through his teeth in imitation of his favorite uncle.

Three maids entered with silver platters of steaming meat, asparagus and colcannon. Phil was surprised to find the last dish—an Irish staple of potatoes, cabbage, scallions, sour cream and butter—in such an august setting. The Troop mess sometimes served it to very good reviews.

Phil concentrated on his plate. Everything was flawless. The chops were redolent with the soft gaminess of lamb, the asparagus somehow crisp yet tender, and the colcannon basically fortified cream cheese and butter.

Harry Hopkins picked at his plate.

When the president had dispatched with his lamb chops, he reached into the breast pocket of his jacket.

"Winston cabled me this morning," he said.

He read from the paper.

"Franklin: American and Aussie masterstroke in the Bismarck Sea a fitting capstone to ten years of inspired leadership."

Harry Hopkins smiled. "Just like Winston to remember the anniversary of your first inauguration."

The president smiled back. "You gifted me a fast friend in him, Harry, but Bismarck Sea is remarkable news."

The day before, the US Eighth and the Royal Australian Air Forces had completed two days of skip bombing a relief convoy bound to reinforce the Japanese garrison on New Guinea. The Japanese had lost twenty fighters, all eight troop transports, four destroyers and nearly 3,000 killed at an Allied cost of two bombers, four fighters and thirteen airmen. *The New York Times* had seized the propaganda initiative, rounding up and reporting Japanese losses of 55 aircraft, 22 ships and 15,000 killed.

Harry Hopkins nodded. "The papers' enthusiasm doesn't diminish the importance of the win, Mr. President."

The president killed his wine and smiled. "We need an enduring tagline, Harry. Something like 'The Battling Bastards of Bataan' or 'The Bruising Bombers of the Bismarck Sea'."

The First Lady put down her fork.

"I guess 'bastards' would be about right, Franklin," she said. "After all, we abandoned them."

The president exhaled slowly. He was no longer smiling.

"Eleanor, it could not be helped. We simply had no one to send to them."

"We have no idea how many of our men in Japanese captivity are even still alive," she answered. "Do our poor boys the dignity of not reducing them to a jingle, please."

Phil suddenly remembered one of his Trooper friends. Charlie Hubbard was one of the funniest guys in the unit. He had been posted to the Philippines in 1940 and no one had heard from him since 1941.

The president tried to restore the mood.

"Eleanor, everyone here recognizes that our boys face a barbaric and implacable foe. We're just trying to enjoy a celebratory dinner with friends."

The First Lady paused before answering.

"Then we should at least remember that thousands of dinners are miserable tonight for mothers whose sons won't be coming home."

No one spoke.

Phil aligned his silverware to tell the staff he was finished and concentrated on his wine. He was no connoisseur, but he knew he would likely never taste better. A friend in Philly had talked about "terroir," the taste of the grape's earth. Savoring the wine's finish, he thought he understood. He was intrigued when the Baked Alaska was placed in front of him. He'd always wondered how they baked ice cream and was curious to try it. The steam from the coffee poured into his cup foretold the perfect cup he had never had.

"I got a letter yesterday, Franklin," Mrs. Roosevelt said in a friendlier tone.

"Of course you did, dear. Everyone loves you."

This drew a cool sidelong glance at Missy LeHand from the First Lady.

"It was from the Nisei."

She mispronounced it "Neesee."

The president leaned back in his wheelchair with an air of resignation.

"I understand that our Japanese friends from the Coast are having a rough go of it."

The First Lady held his eyes for a moment before continuing.

"Apparently, you don't understand, Franklin, because they're not Japanese. They're Americans."

The president showed her the palms of both hands. "Of course, dear," he said. "It was a figure of speech. I'll have Harry see if he can do anything to address their complaint."

"Maybe you'd like to know what it is first?"

"I was told they were unhappy with the lack of qualified teachers in the camp schools?"

"I'm sure that's true. Just like they're probably unhappy about being locked behind barbed wire in the middle of nowhere, having done nothing wrong."

Phil forgot to breathe as he watched the leader of the free world take instruction.

The First Lady continued very quietly. "This is a letter with thousands of signatures, Franklin."

"It's a petition."

"Addressed to me," she said. "Can you guess what they want?"

The president cocked his head slightly. "Please tell me, dear."

"They don't want better food, warmer barracks, or better doctors. They want to fight for this country. They want to wear the uniform and bear the risks and sacrifices."

She drew herself up higher in her chair.

"This for the country that locks them up, that calls them filthy names," she whispered.

The president watched as his wife looked at her lap. Her shoulders began to shake. He took the wheels of his chair in his hands as if to go to her but stopped himself. Instead, he sat motionless, looking almost stricken as he watched her for several long seconds before turning to Harry Hopkins.

"Please make it happen, Harry."

TEA

Honolulu, Hawaii
16 Months After Pearl Harbor

They could have been on a front porch in Kansas but for the carefully raked sand and stone garden fronting the street. Fumi's family were the only Japanese living in the shaded neighborhood of Manoa, high above the city on the slopes of the towering green Pali.

Joe had gotten the invitation to tea in the mail. Fumi's mother had written the invitation in fountain pen on heavy stock engraved with the Ikeda family seal. Surmising Joe's samurai lineage from his last name, Mrs. Ikeda had penned an expedient postscript apologizing for the modesty of the tea ceremony to which he was invited.

In fact, Joe had never seen a tea ceremony, his parents being inclined to coffee and beer.

Surprised and flattered to be the only guest, Joe sat quietly as Fumi and her mother performed the ancient ritual for him. No gesture was small enough to be overlooked. Every last movement was choreographed to connote reverence for the guest and for the bounty on offer. Yet, somehow, mother and daughter imbued the endlessly rehearsed performance with the spontaneity of a fawn.

Joe had been transfixed by Fumi wielding the slivered bamboo whisk. The same hand that could produce an explosive tennis serve held the whisk like an Impressionist's brush and frothed the tea in the cup without touching its sides.

Fumi's mother, however, had eclipsed her daughter. Never once uttering a word, she spent the entire thirty minutes with her eyes averted as she maneuvered delicately from the waist up and filled the small space with gentle authority. Joe found himself anxious for her to like him. He had been surprised at how happy he was to see her lift her eyes in a small smile as she finally passed him his cup.

Taken as he had been by the ritual, he still tasted nothing different in the tea.

After the tea ceremony, Fumi's parents had left them alone and she sat next to Joe in the rocker on the darkened front porch as they looked out over the city lights.

"What are you going to do, Joe?"

Joe had no particular intentions for Fumi, at least no long-term ones. He struggled to compose a suitable answer.

"Well, of course, it's hard to say…"

If Fumi had caught the dodge, she didn't seem to care. She rescued him.

"I mean it. President Roosevelt has approved the formation of a Nisei unit. Every guy I know is joining up."

"Fumi, how does it make sense to go get killed for the same people that see us as their enemy?"

He felt hollow as he said it. No one he actually knew, Japanese or white, regarded him as anything but a friend.

Fumi's eyes narrowed. She leaned in but said nothing.

"They're locking us up. Wouldn't volunteering be a little dramatic?" Joe asked.

"Name one of our friends who's been locked up," Fumi said, cocking her head in question.

She didn't let him answer before continuing. "Besides, that's not the point. This is bigger than you or me."

Joe was tempted to say that getting shot or bombed was bigger than he needed, but Fumi spoke again before he could.

"The Fascists want to plunge the whole world into darkness," she said. "They're trying to undo the Enlightenment. Voltaire, Descartes—they never existed to these people. They don't believe in the dignity of the individual."

Joe had a vision of her in a sunlit parlor parsing the Ascent of Man with her Barnard classmates. He realized he really wasn't ready to debate the world's future with a determined Seven Sisters French major.

He decided to fake flunking the induction physical.

GAMAN

Molokai, Hawaii
17 Months After Pearl Harbor

Even across the water, Joe could see Kiichi's tail thrumming like a dynamo. The dog stood rigid in front of Joe's parents on Kamalo Pier and watched as the ferry brought Joe from Honolulu. The gray of the earthen pier protruded from the dazzling green of windward Molokai into the deep blue of the Pailolo Channel separating Molokai from Maui. Joe had telephoned his parents to say that he was joining up (or at least pretending to try) and he was coming home to say goodbye.

The Horiuchi homestead was a three-room bungalow on a concrete pad set under the trees just beyond the pier. No running water or electricity, but rather a well, kerosene lanterns, and an outhouse.

Joe's room was nearly unchanged, his bed, dresser and desk just as he'd left them. Joe's mother had removed a poster of Betty Grable from the wall and replaced it with Joe's American Legion Scholarship medal. Two modest golf trophies provided the only other adornment.

The front room was the heart of the house. Opening onto a deep front porch under the corrugated steel roof, the space comprised kitchen, dining area and sitting room. Aside from a calendar from Molokai Feed & Grain, most of the wall space was covered with pictures of Joe—a somber first grader scowling from a knot of ragged brown kids on his first day of school, smiling next to his father with his first deer, resplendent in blazer and white ducks on his graduation from Lahainaluna.

Almost everything happened at the scarred and scuffed kitchen table or on the wood-fired range behind it. The opposite side of the room said more, though.

There, a low table set with charcoal linen cushions emblazoned in tiny aqua chrysanthemums was reserved for important occasions. Joe's father had cut the paulownia table top himself and had burnished it by hand to a soft glow with endless applications of tung oil. The wood's intricate grain shimmered in the light from the candle sconces on the wall behind it.

The center of the table held a bucket with several beer bottles on ice. Three places were set, with dishes of ice under smaller plates with fileted raw *fugu*—blowfish. This most-prized Japanese delicacy was fiendishly expensive, if only because its skin, liver and genitalia contain a neurotoxin with no known antidote. Fugu chefs in Japan were rigorously regulated, but Joe's mother had somehow picked up the skill of preparing the fish and occasionally did so for special occasions. She hadn't killed anyone yet.

"We're very proud of you, son," Joe's mother added after saying grace.

Joe didn't really want to discuss his supposedly imminent induction. He concentrated instead on the mythically subtle flavor of the deadly fish. His mother had brushed the filets very lightly with homemade *ponzu*, and the sweet rice wine and *yuzu* vinegar of the sauce was almost all he could taste. The overall effect was, in fact, delicious, but he couldn't help but wonder why people risked death to enjoy it.

Joe's parents sat across from him with their legs folded beneath them. The wall behind them bore a crucifix and a Kwantung Army sword from the Japanese occupation army in Manchuria. The sword was machine-made, a crude send-up of the folded and hammered steel *tama-hagane* blade that still hung in the family's parlor in Buzen at the southernmost tip of Fukuoka. This one was a short grappling blade, a *wakizashi*, which had been all the sword that Joe's father could afford. He kept it oiled and sharp, although it never left the wall.

It was the framed photograph between the sword and the crucifix that drew the eye, though.

A young woman in a nun's habit gazed out into the room from a faded photograph. Even in the harsh folds of her habit, you could see she was beautiful. Mother Marianne Cope would eventually be canonized a saint of the Roman Catholic Church, but to Joe's mother, she was "Mother Marianne," her first boss when she arrived in Hawaii from Japan in 1910 and assumed her duties as a charwoman at the leprosarium on Kalaupapa, Molokai.

The photograph had hung there for as long as Joe could remember. His mother had taught Joe from earliest childhood about her remarkable benefactress. Born Barbara Koob in the Grand Duchy of Hesse, Mother Marianne had emigrated as a little girl to upstate New York, where her family had found prosperity. Pretty, poised and rich, she had nonetheless opted to join the Sisters of Saint Francis.

She was forty-five and running the New York chapter of the order when King Kalakaua of Hawaii put out the call for help for the benighted lepers quarantined on the peninsula of Kalaupapa. Father Damien de Veuster, who would also become a saint of the Roman Catholic Church, had been ministering to the lepers with a small band of brave Belgian priests and monks for ten years. Native Hawaiians, having no natural resistance, had proven dramatically susceptible to foreign infectious diseases. Leprosy in particular, initially borne by Chinese laborer immigrants to the islands, had decimated the populace.

Weakened by their disease, the lepers had been unable to survive unassisted on the desolate peninsula of Kalaupapa, isolated by the world's highest sea cliffs and buffeted by powerful currents and winds. Having helped the lepers of Kalaupapa, Father Damien had finally contracted the illness and was dying from it. Despite their heroic efforts, the small band of clerics needed help.

Sister Marianne decided to provide it.

Fifty orders had refused the call. Leprosy was highly contagious, and incurable. But Sister Marianne had begun her response to King Kalakaua, "I am hungry for the work."

Joe had never met Mother Marianne; she had died just after he was born. But he had heard about her from both parents since he had been old enough to understand kindness. His parents would occasionally take him along when they packed gifts—usually tea cakes or clothes made by Joe's mother—down the sea cliff to the lepers. Joe had always enjoyed the mule ride up and down the cliff face, but he'd been struck early on by how rude some of the lepers could be to the people who were helping them.

When he was seven, his mother had distributed tea cookies to a number of new arrivals to the leprosarium. Joe had watched aghast as a teenage girl, still pretty and unscathed by sores, had knocked his mother's proffered tray into the dirt. Joe's mother had said not a word, but just smiled quietly and took another tray to offer to the next leper in line.

Joe's mother had explained in Japanese, "The young girl is very unhappy, Joe. She had her whole life in front of her and now she's going to die here, away from the people she loves and ruined by that terrible disease. She just couldn't control herself."

When Joe said nothing, she continued.

"Sometimes it's very hard to control yourself. You're sad. You're scared. You're angry. But it's your job always to be in control of yourself —not to let yourself be mean or bad."

Joe hadn't argued, but he had been too young to appreciate the fullness of the lesson. Throughout his way up, though, he'd found people worth following. His father had saved for years from repairing engines and doing odd jobs to buy Joe his first—and only—shotgun, a Parker double barrel 12-gauge that handled like an extension of his arm. Joe's mother never stopped visiting the lepers and making clothes for them. Mr. Alton had spent countless hours quietly explaining schoolwork to countless students, including Joe, when he could have gone home to dinner. Frannie would die before he'd let his mother or Hibiki be made unhappy.

As Joe finished the last of his fugu, his parents looked quietly at him from across the table. Joe decided to deflate the cloying poignancy of the moment.

"Ogata–san is still locked up, I understand?"

Joe's father nodded. "He and others, as well. Very unfortunate."

"Why is everyone so keen to fight for a country that locks up people who've never done anything wrong?" Joe asked.

He drained the last of his beer as his father leaned back and wrinkled his brow.

"Or drops in just to slap me around a little bit?" Joe added.

Joe's father shook his head.

"This is also the country that gave you your home on this island, Lahainaluna, and your career as a sensei, a teacher."

When Joe didn't reply, his father continued.

"In Buzen, you probably would not even have enough to eat."

"It all is just so unfair," Joe managed.

His father shrugged. "Duty is not always fair. You cannot stand by while others sacrifice for what you enjoy."

Joe did not have a riposte. His father turned from the table and did something Joe had never seen him do. He removed the sword from its brackets on the wall. Being careful not to touch the blade, he laid the sword by its sharkskin handle on the paulownia tabletop.

Joe's father and mother were still Japanese subjects. They'd never been allowed to become American citizens. Joe's father's English was still very stilted, but he chose to speak it now.

"Son, this is not your family sword, but you deserve to have it. This is your country. To fight for it now is *gaman*."

Joe had first heard the term from his old kendo teacher. Tired to the point of retching from the interminable kata and sparring, ten-year-old Joe had collapsed, gagging, on the edge of the tatami.

Ogata-san had rallied him with two words. "Gaman, Joe."

The quiet endurance of the unendurable.

Joe had later recognized it in a quote from one his favorite authors. Ernest Hemingway had defined courage as "grace under pressure."

Joe looked at the sword on the table in front of him and realized he could not lie about flunking the induction physical.

PART II

RECRUIT

SWEAT

Camp Shelby, Mississippi
19 Months After Pearl Harbor

*You were the last one at the railing that I could see. Could
you see me waving on the dock?*

Joe was trying not to drip on the letter. His fatigues were
soaked through with his sweat. It stung his eyes and dripped from
the tip of his nose. He sat on his rucksack at the edge of an expanse
of baking red clay surrounded by peanut fields shimmering in the
Mississippi heat. All around him his friends were doing the same
thing—reading the mail that had been delivered in a gunny sack
thrown from the back of an Army deuce-and-a-half truck.

None of the boys are left. Everyone has joined a service.

Joe hated Mississippi and hearing from Fumi almost made it
worse—almost, but not quite. Her letters took him away from the
unremitting heat and the endless road marches of his new home.
The *L'Heure Bleue* Fumi sprinkled on her pages took him back to
the smell of her hair in the flowers and salt breeze he'd left.

Mississippi smelled of mud and manure. Four weeks at
Camp Shelby and he had yet to elicit more than one word at a
time from any of the locals.

The whole territory is talking about the unit. I'm so proud of you.

Joe imagined his return to her after, hopefully, brief and uneventful service in uniform. Her tears of relief would soak the chest of his tunic. Her joyful sobs would rack her beautifully configured body pressed urgently to him.

In the meantime, he and the rest of his company had to cover another eight miles. He folded the letter carefully and slipped it into his rucksack. As he stood, he hoisted the ruck over his head and onto his shoulders in one practiced motion. With the rest of his squad, he fell into the line of soldiers now walking into the sun on the single-lane track of packed earth.

His feet didn't hurt anymore. That would come later when he gingerly removed the socks saturated with blood from his burst blisters. But his shoulders never stopped aching. Fifty pounds of water, food, and ammunition sawed his pack straps into his shoulders with each footfall. The constant cramp in his shoulders was more insistent than the repeated punishment to the soles of his feet hitting the unforgiving road. What most affronted, though, was his gun.

The M-1 was a crude, heavy thing. With its parts machine-stamped instead of hand-finished like his Parker's, it weighed half again as much as the shotgun, which had two barrels. Its wood was tacky with linseed oil, not painstakingly rubbed by hand to a lacquer finish like the shotgun's. Mainly, Joe just couldn't figure out how to carry it comfortably. He couldn't hold it and swing his arms in rhythm with his feet. He couldn't sling it over a shoulder without holding the strap and ruining his rhythm. Slinging it over his head and one shoulder was just too awkward with the rucksack, so he alternated shoulders and swung one elbow in time against his swinging free arm. This seemed cumbersome and embarrassing until he realized everyone else was doing the same thing.

Camp Shelby had become a blur of calisthenics, weapons instruction, too little sleep, bland haole food, and marching.

"The army values your feet, and your rifle. We may have planes and tanks and trucks, but they'll never be enough without the guys that walk to the enemy and shoot him."

Since introducing himself to the trainees, First Sergeant Parrish had shown a commendable economy of words. Joe had never seen him without a plug of chew between his lip and his gums—even when he was eating or drinking. His flat, prolonged vowels placed him from somewhere in the Southeast. His fatigues hung from a frame devoid of nonessential flesh.

Joe and his friends had questioned the need to march constantly, ever further and with increasingly heavy loads. The first sergeant had set them right.

"Marksmanship, hand to hand, demolition—they're all important. But the man who can walk forever, over any terrain, with any load you give him, is the man who'll put the steel to the enemy."

Now the first sergeant walked alongside the column of marching men, carrying the same load, but wearing a .45 instead of an M-1. He was just as sweat-soaked as everyone else, but he seemed fresh, his gait long and relaxed as he ate the route with his feet.

Suddenly, two boys in the line were scuffling.

"Fuck off, Kotonk," one was yelling as he shoved another, a "Buddhahead," backward and off his feet. The assailant pressed his advantage, drawing back to kick with his heavy combat boot. In their first three weeks at Shelby, the trainees had fractured between those from Hawaii and those from the mainland. After frequent fights, the former had christened the latter "Kotonks" for the sound of a coconut hitting an empty head. The latter had returned the favor by calling the Hawaiians "Buddhaheads" for their awkward rustic haircuts.

Now these two feinted and parried around each other, each waiting for his moment. Neither got it. Instead, the first sergeant, without breaking stride, sailed between them and sent each to the dirt with a resounding slap.

The whole column had stopped now, the line of marching men becoming a jumble of aimless onlookers. The first sergeant faced the two antagonists with his hands on his hips. The entire platoon had gone silent.

"Do not ever make me hit a soldier again. Not one of my own."

The expressions on the faces around him confirmed that he would not again be so burdened.

He paused for several moments in silence before slipping his ruck from his shoulders and dropping it where he stood.

"Bring it in. Take five."

The platoon gathered in front of him as he settled onto his ruck and shook a cigarette from his somewhat damp pack of Luckies.

"Smoke 'em if you got 'em."

He held his Zippo to his cigarette and then threw his own pack of cigarettes to a soldier who'd turned to beg one from a friend. The company settled as he drew the rich velvet of his first puff deep into the furthest recesses of his lungs.

"Why are you here, men?"

The men were not prepared for the Socratic method. No one spoke.

He tried again. "You're all volunteers. Why did you volunteer for the infantry?"

When still no one answered, he looked at the closest soldier, a cane cutter from Hilo, Joe Tsuji.

"Tsuji, why did you volunteer?"

Tsuji looked almost angry at being forced to speak, but he finally managed.

"It's everyone's fight, sergeant."

"Is it?" wondered the first sergeant. Then he said, "How about Suzuki here? He volunteered out of Manzanar. That's a prison camp. Why is it his fight?"

Tsuji shrugged after a moment. "I guess you should ask him, First Sergeant."

The first sergeant turned to Suzuki.

"What about it, Suzuki? Why did you volunteer to wear the same uniform as the guys keeping your family behind barbed wire?"

Suzuki shuffled uncomfortably on his ruck and looked at his feet. Finally, Suzuki looked up.

"I figured this would have to be better than the camp."

No one said anything.

Suzuki looked slowly to the ranks of filthy, sweaty, exhausted men to either side of him. Finally, he shrugged his shoulders.

"It seemed like a good idea at the time."

The first sergeant smiled for the first time in anyone's memory.

Everyone was smiling. Some were even laughing.

The first sergeant sat still for a moment, taking in the first time both halves of the platoon had agreed on anything. When he finally spoke, he did so in a parade ground snarl—muted, but clearly audible to everyone there.

"It doesn't matter why you volunteered. You're here. You're not just Infantry. You're the 442nd Infantry. You volunteered even though half the country hates you. The whole country is watching you."

No one was laughing now.

"You learn to work together or you fail—if you live at all. Learn that no one on this earth is more important than the man next to you, than the men around you."

He let that register.

"The Axis are waiting to butcher you. The inbreds around here think you should be POWs. You don't need any more enemies."

The fights stopped.

LIEUTENANT LYNCH

Camp Shelby, Mississippi
20 Months After Pearl Harbor

Joe, some of these boys are so broken—and so young.

Joe had grown to expect Fumi's letters every couple of days. He found himself almost despondent when the daily gunny sack of platoon mail failed to yield a letter for two straight days.

Honestly, I volunteered at Tripler because I thought I'd look nice in candy stripes. Now, I can't imagine not helping out. Most of these soldiers and Marines coming in from the islands have no one here.

Joe sat on the edge of his bunk in his platoon squad bay at Camp Shelby. Shaded by trees, the barrack's high ceilings and profusion of open windows afforded the closest thing to comfort on offer. The day's physical training had wrung him out, but less so than two months earlier. Most importantly, his feet and shoulders no longer ached.

Joe smiled inwardly at the mental image of Fumi crisp in her pink striped nurse's uniform, gliding brightly through the hospital corridors. He could do without dwelling on the injuries of her patients, however.

One of them is a really handsome Marine Lieutenant from Baltimore, Kevin Lynch. He was medevacked out of Bouganville and he has not said a single word since he arrived.

Joe had read about battle fatigue, the affliction of soldiers for whom the unremitting stress of combat had simply proven to be too much. In World War I, it had been called shell shock because most of its victims had failed under constant, prolonged artillery bombardment. Joe understood the condition to be elastic, rendering some victims merely nervous while the most grievously afflicted could be left catatonic.

Lieutenant Lynch went to the Naval Academy. He's got a picture of a lovely girl at his bedside, but no one has ever come in to visit him. Every day, his orderly wheels him in a chair out to a huge banyan tree on the front lawn and lights cigarettes for him. The head nurse asked me to keep them company.

Joe remembered the tree, broad with a dense canopy and cavernous shade underneath. The tree would rustle gently in the breeze off the ocean as myna birds called in the branches—a nice place for a smoke.

I started to accompany the two of them, lighting the lieutenant's cigarettes and talking about anything pleasant that comes to mind. His only reaction is to take the proffered cigarette and draw on it without a word.

Joe pictured her ministering gently to the man.

Last Friday, though, the new Navy psychiatrist dropped by.

Joe pictured a portly man with glasses.

You would really like Ensign Ishii. He's right out of a residency at Johns Hopkins and he played water polo for Stanford.

Joe began to wonder about the glasses.

He carries himself with easy assurance but could not be nicer to everyone here.

Joe really didn't need to read any more about this particular water walker.

He is so handsome in his lab coat. He looks like a boxer walking into the ring in his warmup robe.

Joe was about to put the letter aside, but the next line stopped him.

It was just awful. I felt terrible for him. He walked up to us smiling just as I handed the lieutenant a cigarette. He took a knee in front of the lieutenant and was about to introduce himself when the lieutenant just started to shriek. I mean really shriek. People on the other side of Kapiolani could hear him. Ensign Ishii recoiled just an inch in spite of himself, but mainly he just looked utterly pierced. I felt so sad for him. Later, one of the lieutenant's friends came by the ward to apologize. "Sir," he said, "please don't take it personally. The lieutenant was left out on the line too long. Every night, screaming Japanese charging out of the darkness, slicing with those swords. He lost a lot of his Marines, but he held the position for days." Joe, you would have been so proud of the way he handled it. He just held up his hands and shook his head. "Please don't apologize, Marine," he said. "It's not the lieutenant's fault that I look like the enemy."

BETTY

Camp Shelby, Mississippi
24 Months After Pearl Harbor

"The S-Mine is the Germans' most common anti-personnel mine. They call it 'Bouncing Betty.' It will bounce out of the ground and explode a yard in the air—taking your balls and killing everyone within twenty-five yards."

First Sergeant Parrish shook an innocuous looking can that could have held baked beans. Three little prongs protruded from its top.

"You explode it by stepping on and then off one of these prongs. A preliminary charge propels it out of the ground to waist height, where the main charge detonates and sends 350 ball bearings in a 365-degree radius."

Joe and the rest of his platoon knelt or stood in a semicircle before the first sergeant. Joe had been happy that the day's training called for instruction instead of another ruck march, even though Mississippi was suffused in winter gray and the air was brisk. Joe and his friends were no longer exhausted at the end of each day's training. Now, they were only tired.

"The mine's primary purpose is to restrict movement—to force infantry into corridors where they can be met by artillery or enfilade fire."

Joe tried not to visualize the alternatives.

"Today, each one of you is going to defuse one."

With that, the first sergeant motioned the men to several long tables painted red and bearing S-Mines at five-foot intervals. An Ordnance Corps NCO stood in front of each mine.

"Line up in columns of four on each mine."

Joe noticed another red table behind the rest with some thirty-plus mines. What followed was thirty minutes of the closest attention he had ever paid to a lesson.

Each ordnance NCO slowly and very gently took a mine and unscrewed its cap. Using a bayonet tip, each then depressed and disengaged the arming spring under the cap. When they were done, the first sergeant continued.

"Once defused, these are inert. They're harmless. You can kick them and they won't go off."

Joe wondered at the circumstance that would actually impel him to defuse one of the things in the field. Wouldn't it be simpler, he asked himself, just to exit the area once they encountered one?

He was certain the command had already disarmed all the mines by removing their charges. Everyone was cautious to a fault, however, as he took one in his hands and followed the procedure under the watchful eye of the attending instructor.

Joe was third in line, but his hands still trembled as he took the cap between his thumb and middle finger and started to twist. The handle of his bayonet was slippery with his sweat as he pushed his bayonet into the resulting space. He took at least a minute lightly probing with the knife tip before he encountered the plate connected to the arming spring. He exhaled when the gentle pressure of his bayonet tip produced a quiet, but clearly audible, *click*.

"Put it on the white table and you're dismissed until noon chow," said his instructor, gesturing to a nearby table freshly painted white and covered haphazardly with a dozen defused mines.

Joe decided to retrieve the jerry can from his bivouac and fill it from the water buffalo, a mobile water tank, parked 300 yards away.

He was headed back to his two-man pup tent, thinking there was just no way comfortably to carry five gallons of water in one hand, when the first mine went off—a flat, resounding slap of air and sound from just over the gentle rise separating him from the training site. It was followed instantly by a second, louder boom which didn't end, but instead built into a ragged, syncopated roar of sympathetic detonations.

Joe instinctively dropped the jerry can and covered his face as he dove to the ground. He didn't see the pulsing flashes like lightning at the edge of the rise, but the earth beneath him shook to the percussive beat of a drum riff from hell. He noticed the taste of dirt in his mouth before he noticed the stillness that followed the explosions.

He lay still for a moment trying to decide whether he was hurt anywhere, before slowly pushing himself to his feet. Without deciding to, he started to run toward the silence.

He smelled the blast before cresting the rise—a thin, acrid scent of scorch. Worse than the smell of the blast was the sight of it—a naked, smoking circle of black dirt with debris and red stripes radiating from its outer edges to pieces of equipment and men strewn for seventy-five yards.

Joe stood on the rise unable to will his feet to move. His stomach lurched and he left his breakfast at his feet without realizing it. He could not say how long he stood there before he started to hear the crying. He finally put one foot in front of the other when he heard the first shriek.

He wanted to help somehow, but he'd taken only ten steps when he nearly tripped over Frank Kanemitsu sitting and staring dumbly at what remained of his left leg pulsing into the dirt the brightest red Joe had ever seen. Without thinking, Joe imitated his first aid instruction, removing his web belt as he knelt beside Frank and tightening the belt around his thigh in a tourniquet. He took Frank's shoulders and shook them.

"Leave this on, Frank. Don't touch it."

Frank just stared into the middle distance. Joe shook him again.

"Tell me you understand."

Frank met his eyes and nodded slowly.

Joe took in the scene. Men splotched in red were moving, some walking unsteadily, others crawling. Four or five were already on their knees trying to help others, many of whom were not moving at all and some of whom would never move again. The scene was chaotic—men sprinting from over the rise into the blast site, men shouting questions or exhorting others, and above it all, a chorus of sobs and shrieks.

Joe moved from one fallen man to the next, applying pressure to wounds, checking those who were unresponsive for a pulse, eliciting a response from the others. He would not realize until after the ambulance and medics arrived that everyone around him who could was doing the same thing.

The last man he approached was clearly beyond help—the back of his fatigue tunic shredded and the ground around him soggy with blood. The man was utterly limp as Joe took one shoulder to turn him over. Joe started to cry when he saw the first sergeant's chevrons on the sleeve.

BLESSING

Manhattan, New York
25 Months After Pearl Harbor

"**Y**ou're infantry now, men, and you're going to show that you're damned good infantry. In fact, you have no choice. You've chosen a motto—Go for Broke—that promises absolute mayhem to the enemy."

Colonel Pence was addressing the whole hastily gathered battalion in the cavernous concourse of Manhattan's Penn Station after they'd detrained from Mississippi.

On the interminable train trip from San Francisco to Camp Shelby, Joe had decided that the American landmass could not get much bigger. The trip to New York had proven him wrong. He and Sparky had shared a rail car with sixty other guys. The Buddhaheads and the Kotonks had gambled and regaled each other with their soon-to-be exploits in New York, but everyone had been reduced to awed silence at the first sight of the silvered city skyline on the horizon.

Joe looked up at the impossibly high ceiling of the concourse and around him over a sea of drab khaki bearing 750 smiling yellow faces.

"We sail for Europe tomorrow morning. You'll be billeted tonight on Governor's Island. The USO Hall near the Staten Island Ferry terminus is hosting a dance for you this evening."

The NCOs barely needed to guide the men as they formed up by platoon on Seventh Avenue for the short march to their buses at the Port Authority Terminal. The street was crowded with the usual crush of New Yorkers going about their business. They paused, however, at the sight of hundreds of diminutive soldiers with Japanese faces filling their street.

America had been at war for over two years. The daily papers and radio bulletins never failed to chronicle the loss and sacrifice of the forces of freedom, or the depravity of their foes. Everyone had someone in the fight, and no one misunderstood the need to crush the Axis.

Joe squared his shoulders against his pack straps and weapon as the men around him dressed their ranks in silence.

No one, soldier or civilian, said a word. A pocket of midtown Manhattan, perhaps for the first time since the Dutch stole it from the Indians, was quiet at midday.

Then someone on the sidewalk clapped. Slowly, unevenly, the clapping grew, traveling up the sidewalks and finally echoing off the surrounding buildings. Joe could barely hear the command "Forward March" as they set off in crisp cadence.

Suddenly, every man in the column was keenly aware of the distinctive unit patch adorning his left shoulder: the Torch of Freedom in white against a field of blue bordered in red.

Despite himself, Joe could feel the fullness in his throat and chest as he took in the cheering onlookers. He'd come to learn at Camp Shelby that not all mainland haoles regarded the Nisei as enemies. One local, a rancher named Earl Grimes, had essentially adopted the entire regiment, repeatedly hosting large groups of the men for pit barbeques at his nearby home.

Joe noticed a middle-aged couple on the edge of the sidewalk. They could've been Mr. and Mrs. Alton, twenty years older. They both stood still and straight in sober gray flannel, but Joe was looking at the husband's shoes, which were not unlike Joe's solid Alden Bluchers, but burnished to a high gloss. He absently noted that the wife was stepping off the sidewalk and closer to the marching column. Then he saw the black armbands on their sleeves. He realized she was looking directly at him and he met her eyes as she spoke.

"God bless you, Go for Broke."

PENANCE

Manhattan, New York
25 Months After Pearl Harbor

"**M**en, you've trained hard together. You've come together as a unit. You've taken casualties before even getting to Theater. You've earned the right to enjoy yourselves and God has provided this marvelous metropolis of New York for you to do so."

Captain Wilson, the newly assigned regimental chaplain, was Episcopalian. He addressed Joe and about fifty other soldiers on the afterdeck of the Governor's Island Ferry. Joe's battalion had deposited their gear in the billets on Governor's Island and were now returning to the Staten Island terminal at the foot of Manhattan. Joe could not agree with the chaplain more. He'd imagined his night in the world's greatest city for weeks. The chaplain lost him, however, with his follow up.

"Remember, men, that you represent your unit, your families and your people. The New Yorkers will remember warmly your comportment tonight as Christian gentlemen."

Aside from the fact that a lot of the guys were actually Buddhist, Joe didn't know when or even if he would return to New York. He did know that he'd had little opportunity to spend his soldier's wage at Camp Shelby and New York offered the best opportunity of his life to enjoy food, drink...and women.

Diamond Jim Brady, a New York railroad mogul, had been notorious for his monumental commitment to food that was superlative in quantity as well as quality. Joe planned to take dinner at one of Brady's favorite haunts, Delmonico's, and eat some of his favorite food, seared rib eye and oysters on the half shell. Joe had read that the Long Island and New England oysters were famously sweet and firm. He concluded they must be since Mr. Alton had rhapsodized about New England oysters, but no one seemed to seek the oysters to be found in Hawaii's tidal estuaries.

He would open the meal with the cocktail New York had given to the world, the martini. He remembered William Powell languidly shaking the drink for Myrna Loy in *The Thin Man*. Joe wanted his dry as sunlight. Gin chilled almost to syrup with just a drop of vermouth, shaken over ice and poured straight up into a frozen glass. Finally, a tiny cocktail onion.

First, though, he needed a date.

The USO had repurposed a shipping broker's office across from the Staten Island terminal for the thousands of soldiers shipping out from lower Manhattan to points east. Joe, Sparky, Harry, and Frankie emerged from the terminal and made for its entrance.

Joe expected a good evening. He was fit enough to walk through walls and sharp in his pressed "Pinks," the Class A uniform, with its distinctive shoulder patch.

Four abreast, they strode through the wide doorway into the open room that had previously been crowded with brokers matching cargo and vessels listed on the blackboards that covered the walls. Now the blackboards were draped in red, white and blue bunting and there were flowers everywhere. Roses, carnations, delphiniums, laburnums… The whole place was heavy with the fragrance of the blooms. Joe remembered the sea of plumeria leis that was his Lahainaluna graduation.

He took it all in. Tables of hors d'oeuvres and pastries, a swing band quietly warming up in one corner and, at the far end, the bar. Joe failed to note the handsome collection of bottles behind the bar. Just in front of the bar stood three women.

Lavinia Spetz and two of her Smith classmates had volunteered to organize the party. The flowers, the food, the band, the thirty other women helping out or standing around— all were her doing. She was surveying her work when the boys walked in. Her hair was only slightly darker than her pearls and it fell in a dense cascade to her shoulders. Her chin was up and her smile was nearly as bright as her green eyes that riveted Joe from twenty yards.

Joe was not discouraged by the enlisted rank of corporal on his shoulder. He already knew her. He'd seen every movie with Katherine Hepburn.

He stepped into the room towards her and realized with a start that she was smiling directly at him. Almost unconsciously, he stood a little taller and returned her smile. As he crossed the room with his friends just behind him, he pondered the right opening line. He was gliding over the parquet, and she just kept smiling, watching him without moving a muscle. He was dizzy with command. They were the only two people in the room.

Suddenly, she was there right in front of him, cocking her lovely head very slightly and extending her hand to him with a drink. He took it, holding just for an instant her perfectly poised fingers as he beheld the best reason he had yet found for going to war.

"Are you ready for the best six seconds of your life?" he asked.

Her face froze. She didn't stop smiling, but she held the words she'd been about to say.

Lavinia's brother was a West Pointer who had just graduated from Artillery Basic. Still smiling, but somewhat ruefully, she shook her head.

"Way to fire for effect, soldier."

Joe had his Pittsburghed Delmonico steak and two dozen Wellfleet oysters that night, accompanied by four of the best martinis he was likely ever to taste—the first two, anyway. But his dates were Sparky, Harry, and Franny. They, at least, laughed at his jokes.

PART III

SOLDIER

DUEL

Grosseto, Italy
Rome—Arno Campaign
30 Months and 2 Weeks After Pearl Harbor

"The Germans have registered the coordinates of every hilltop, every ridgeline, every road or trail junction – and they've set up converging artillery on all of them. What they can't hit, they've mined."

The 100th had been fighting in Italy since Anzio, eight months. Major Gillespie commanded one of its battalions and now he was explaining to the new Nisei arrivals what they would find here. The Italians had surrendered and were out of the war, but the Germans had occupied Italy for precisely that eventuality.

"They've established their strong points on the high ground and they build their positions well—deep, with lots of concrete or timber reinforcement."

Joe listened and wondered, not for the first time, at the wisdom of his earlier spasm of volunteerism. He had yet to see the war—at least, the fighting of it. In the week since they'd landed at Civitavecchia, he'd seen the chaos of the port and the teeming poverty of the city. He'd envisioned lush olive orchards, stately columned buildings and dusky, classically configured— and possibly grateful?—women. The trucks that carried them up to Grosseto in the Apennine foothills, however, revealed only a succession of shattered dun-colored mountain towns with skinny, ragged residents.

442 was part of the Allied push to clear Italy beneath the Apennines of the Germans. 442 would fight north from the Mediterranean through the Tuscan foothills to Florence.

Joe had been assigned to M "Mike" Company of 2nd Battalion—Heavy Weapons. This meant mortars, the infantry's ubiquitous indirect fire weapon for lobbing explosives onto enemy positions. Each round was a small explosive-filled rocket. The soldier would cut a wad of the propellant to adjust distance and cram it onto the rocket's base. The soldier would then drop the rocket into a tube with a detonating pin in the bottom and the exploding propellant would expel the round back out of the tube. Knobs affixed to the tube would enable the soldier to adjust the angle and direction of the tube and direct the round to the target.

The mortar was the most prodigious casualty producer in an infantry formation, but it had to be carried. Joe had been made a mortarman because he was tall and, presumably, could more easily bear the punishing load. As a corporal, he led a team of four, comprising two teams manning a mortar apiece. Each man carried his personal weapon, usually an M-1, as well as a share of the team's mortar components and rounds. As the tallest, Joe drew the heaviest, and most cumbersome, component—the steel baseplate.

The load was no problem as it sat between Joe's feet in the bed of the deuce-and-a-half lumbering up the highway from Grosseto into the hills. It became one as soon as they reached the jumping-off point for the push on the town of Sassetta. Mike Company was supporting 2nd Battalion's assault on the high ground south of Sassetta. They would walk the rest of the way uphill.

Camp Shelby and its environs had been endlessly flat. Joe had climbed hills hunting deer and goat throughout his boyhood. Then, however, he'd only carried a rifle, several bullets and a scout knife, and a canteen in the summer. Today his pack seemed impossibly heavy as soon as he stepped off the road and started up the parched hillside. Fifty pounds of rifle ammunition, C-rations, shelter half, socks and water became seventy-five with the baseplate. A full canteen and several grenades and ammunition clips festooned his web belt, adding to the load. Joe looked around for a place to stow his wakizashi, which was tied dramatically to one side of his pack, but there was none. It only weighed two pounds anyway.

The next two hours would be the worst of Joe's life up to that point.

Each step was a struggle. The summer heat pressed Joe into the slope before him. No swinging shoulders in rhythm with his gait. Rather, he lurched from one foot to the other as his pack threatened to pull him back down the hill. He was distressed to discover he was out of breath after twenty yards.

He quickly developed a method. He simply fixed his eyes on the crest of the hill, secure in the knowledge that everyone else was as miserable as he. Each step became one step closer to relief. The worst was therefore always behind him.

This approach sufficed for the sixty minutes until he reached the crest—and saw another crest farther away. Each ascent was followed by a shorter descent into a ravine and a longer ascent of the next ridge. The descents were nearly as bad as the ascents as Joe struggled not to roll downhill. He took some little comfort in seeing some of the other guys actually doing so.

From the truck, the hills had seemed modest. *How many successive ravines could there be?* After two hills, he was breathing in ragged gasps that everyone could hear, and his legs were quivering from the effort.

He took to watching his platoon leader, the lieutenant or LT, and his radio telephone operator, the RTO. The latter was never farther than two yards from the former. They were 200 yards in front of Joe and each time they stopped and took a knee was a chance for Joe to do the same. Each time the RTO passed the LT the radiotelephone receiver, Joe silently prayed for an order from battalion or company to halt. The order never came. Instead, the two would take a knee for a minute before standing again to continue the trip. Joe found himself wishing for contact—anything to stop the climb.

He got his wish.

The LT and the RTO had each taken a knee when they suddenly disappeared in a tight eruption of black smoke. Joe heard the muffled report of the explosion an instant later and recognized it as the same made by his own mortar. Everyone dove for the dirt. Joe opened his chin on the grit but kept his eyes on the spot where his lieutenant had been, staring dully at the dissipating smoke and the corona of body parts across the blackened ground. The next blast jarred him back to awareness.

Suddenly, the hillside was alive with mortar bursts, each within seconds of the last and landing farther down the slope. The German mortarman was walking his rounds down the line of advancing infantrymen. Joe forced himself to ignore the approaching bursts and the men bolting out of their path or seeking cover. He ignored, too, the men who were not moving at all. Instead, he scanned the ridgeline in front of them, a barren expanse of brown grass broken here and there with a sad bush or tree. Out in front of his own column, nothing moved. He kept looking, panning slowly from side to side, starting at the top and working downslope.

He had covered the crest and was working back across the face of the slope just below when something made him stop. As a boy on Molokai, Joe had hunted his family's food. He could read a landscape for clues of game that he could not even describe without conscious deliberation. He discovered his gift served him just as well in a battlescape. At 300 yards, the scraggly oak just below the crest was still, unless watched very closely and at length. Every few seconds, the sparse leaves in its sparse branches trembled very slightly.

Joe had not even registered the discrepant feature when he yelled at his teammate, Barney Hakushu.

"Barney, set the rounds for 300 yards."

Joe started to scuttle backward, crab-like, across the slope until he found a slight depression in the ground.

"Give me the tube and keep passing me the rounds."

Barney was confused. The baseplate remained tied to Joe's pack.

"What about the baseplate?"

Joe had never heard either one of his parents swear and Mr. Alton had decried the habit as the refuge of the inarticulate. Joe decided inarticulate was better than dead.

"Fuck the baseplate, Barney."

Joe understood that a mortar's accuracy depended on its proper use, but he could not bring himself to adjust knobs against numbers while the Germans' mortar bursts fell ever closer. Barney opened his mouth to argue, but Joe stopped him.

"Now, goddammit. Keep them coming."

Shoving the base of the tube into the dirt between his knees, Joe began to toggle the mouth of the tube at a 45-degree angle away from himself against his line of sight to the tell-tale tree. He started to feed the proffered rounds into the tube with his right hand as he watched them land and made tiny adjustments to the attitude of the tube with his left.

Joe carried earplugs in his breast pocket and realized he'd forgotten to insert them when he felt the tiny pinprick of pain in his eardrum with the first launch. No time to stop. He guided the tube by feel as he launched the rounds every few seconds and watched them land. Barney was a blur of motion next to him as he cut the propellant and laid each prepared round at Joe's side.

If he'd taken time to think, Joe would have been surprised by his accuracy. His first round had fallen sixty yards in front and slightly left of his objective. He steadily brought the rounds closer as he adjusted direction and angle so minutely that he forgot to breathe. Joe could walk rounds, too.

Had he not been so intent on guiding his own rounds, Joe would have noticed that his adversary had abandoned the rest of the slope. The German's rounds were now landing all around Joe. In his first thirty seconds at war, Joe had started a counter-battery duel.

By now, all of Joe's rounds were landing close enough to the tree to keep it covered in smoke. Joe kept dropping rounds into the smoke until he realized Barney was shaking his shoulder and shouting in his ear.

"You took him out, Joe. He's stopped shooting. You killed the cocksucker!"

The chaplain would later assure the boys that they must feel no regret or personal recrimination in their bloodletting, that it was God's work. Joe knew that to be true, but he'd always wondered whether he might belabor killing a man. He discovered he didn't—at least not this one.

88

Grosseto, Italy
30 Months and 2 Weeks After Pearl Harbor

Joe's pack felt almost refreshingly light when the platoon resumed the climb behind the platoon sergeant—perhaps because the load he shared with Barney was twenty mortar rounds lighter. They had not covered 100 yards when he heard a low ululating moan in the sky which ended with a muffled bang somewhere off to his left.

Krupp had designed the 88-mm recoilless rifle for use against aircraft, but the Germans had repurposed it for use against just about everything. Easily moved, maintained and fired, it would become the most recognized—and feared—artillery piece of the war. Joe and his friends were feeling the application of the 88 to the Germans' meticulously prepared firing grids. The sound alone was terrifying and sent everyone scrambling for cover, bringing to a halt any semblance of an advance.

Suddenly, the sky was filled with eerie moans and shell bursts were erupting all around the slope in front of Joe. His first thought was to get away, to bolt in the only direction free of the terrifying explosions—downhill. Instead, however, he dove onto the ground and willed himself deeper into the dirt beneath him. He couldn't stand the noise, ever louder and shaking the air and the earth around him harder with each blast. He knew one would find him very soon, but still, he could not move. Instead, he just lay there staring at the few blades of grass under his nose and praying for it to stop.

"Up. Get the fuck up and over that rise."

Joe was shocked and angered at this intrusion – shouted into his ear with a resounding slap to his helmet. He decided to ignore the speaker before the voice registered as his platoon sergeant's. He was about to shift to all fours when Ernie Sakai saved him the trouble and hauled him to his feet. Joe bolted for the rise, but not before grabbing Barney's ruck strap and pulling him along.

The rise was one edge of a shallow ravine that ran straight up the slope. Its depression lay just below the line of the 88s' fire. Neither Joe nor Barney felt his pack as they flew like wide receivers upslope toward the beckoning shelter of the rise. All around them, their friends were doing the same as Ernie pulled the remaining stragglers off the ground and yelled at everyone to make for the ravine. Not everyone could hear him anymore.

Joe and Barney huddled in the deepest, although still not very deep, part of the ravine. They crouched there, breathing through their mouths in deep gasps as they waited for Ernie to direct them. Joe's breathing was just starting to subside when he noticed the large wet stain in the crotch of Barney's pants. As he noted the unfairness of this indignity, he realized that Barney was staring back at the crotch of his own pants.

Ernie did not disappoint.

"We're going to use this ravine to climb the slope," he said. "Everyone in staggered formation behind me."

The men began to follow Ernie up the ravine at a low crouch in an uneven spread. No one spoke and they scanned the higher ground before them as the 88s continued to moan and burst on either side, but duller now. Ernie moved deliberately, his .45 Thompson "Tommy Gun" submachine gun alive in his hands as his head swiveled from side to side like a fighter pilot's. The platoon was no less deliberate as it trailed behind toward the crest.

Twenty minutes of this slow march brought them to within a hundred yards of the top. The soldier three behind Ernie felt rather than heard the quiet *snick* of the arming pin on a Bouncing Betty under his foot. Everyone within ten yards heard the click, but the entire platoon heard the soldier as he froze to the spot and screamed, "Mine!"

No one moved—except Ernie. Very slowly, almost painfully, he pivoted on both feet and began to retrace his boot prints back to the stricken man. Private Tetsuo "Tits" Takashi was an alabaster rendition of open-mouthed terror.

Ernie spoke quietly. "Easy, Tits. You're gonna be okay."

Tits did not move as Ernie knelt at his feet. No one else had moved, either.

"I need a rock, a big one."

Still, no one moved. Joe and Barney looked on from fifty yards. Ernie spoke again.

"Someone follow your footprints to a big rock."

When still no one moved, Ernie started to look around as he pulled his bayonet from his web belt. Joe suddenly realized what he was doing. Back at Camp Shelby, the ordnance instructors had shown them how to help a soldier off an armed mine. It had seemed impossibly difficult to Joe and he assumed he'd never see anyone actually try it.

Ernie fixed on a larger rock among the scree lining the bottom of the ravine.

"Larry, you've got a good one to your left. Pick it up and pass it up the line."

Private Lawrence Tanaka's parents had just started catechism classes at the Dole plantation on Lanai when he was born. Larry's mother had loved the story of the saint venerated for his kindness to animals, but her English was still limited and she mistakenly recalled him to be known as "Lawrence of Assisi."

Larry picked up the twenty-pound rock and passed it to the next man. When the rock reached Ernie, he took it in both hands and placed it between his knees.

"Everyone follow your footprints away from me seventy-five yards."

For the next five minutes, the men described a slow retreat back down the gully.

Finally, Ernie leaned forward with his bayonet. "Stay still, Tits. Keep some pressure on the pin. I need to get my blade between your boot and the pin."

Tits did not need to be told. He didn't even look down as Ernie got to work. As if he were restoring a Renaissance painting, Ernie began to work the tip of his bayonet very slowly from side to side as he pushed it under the boot, careful to point the blade slightly upwards. When he thought he felt the tip of the arming pin under his blade, he spoke.

"Don't step off. Just slowly drag your foot off."

Tits did as instructed, and finally looked down to see the mine next to his foot with the bayonet held over its center.

"Now retrace your steps back to the other guys."

Tits complied, trembling, leaving Ernie with one hand holding the bayonet in place, alone.

Joe looked on from his safe remove as Ernie manhandled the rock in his other hand and laid it very carefully across the blade. Finally, Ernie stopped. Very gently he released the rock. When nothing happened, he very slowly opened his other hand on the handle of his bayonet. No one was breathing.

Ernie's impromptu construction sat between his knees. After a moment, his frame visibly relaxed and he started to look over his shoulder. Joe could just see Ernie's smile when he heard a metallic pop followed by a white flash and a sharply sibilant bang.

The blast that would have atomized Tits blew Ernie in two.

442 had its first hero.

MG 42

Grosseto, Italy
30 Months, 2 Weeks and 1 Hour After Pearl Harbor

There was no time to mourn Ernie, or any others of the day's fallen. They had to take the high ground before the push on Sassetta. The stunned silence following Ernie's disintegration had finally been broken when Joe found himself speaking.

"We've got to climb up this gully. They told us how to move through mines."

No one disagreed, so he continued.

"No one step outside a footprint. The lead guy crawls on his belly, probing the ground in front of him with his bayonet. Everyone else follows his path."

Again, no one disagreed, but no one moved, either.

"You're the lead guy, Conrad. We've got less than a hundred yards."

Private Koichi "Conrad" Itoh finally sank to his knees, took out his bayonet, and started, very carefully, to prod the ground in front of him to a ninety-degree radius. The men made the ridge in twenty minutes.

Joe emerged from the gully to find everyone gathered, looking down on Sassetta below. The ridge on which they now stood climbed for another half mile to a gentle peak. No one seemed to be in charge, so Joe spoke again.

"We need to clear the way to that peak, then send a runner back to Company for orders."

This last bit provoked some stony looks, so he added, "Or wait there."

When still no one spoke, he continued.

"We'll take the lee of the slope away from the 88s."

Joe found himself leading three other soldiers toward the peak as the remainder stayed in place waiting for direction from a sergeant rather than a corporal.

Joe wondered whether the rest of his company had secured their portions of the high ground. The men were fanned out unevenly behind him so as to limit casualties if they took fire again. Joe was keeping abeam of what appeared to be a goat or sheep trail when the beaten dirt forty yards out front erupted in a welter of dust and debris followed immediately by a high-pitched sound like silk tearing—but much louder.

The MG 42, the belt-fed light machine gun of the German infantry squad, fired twenty-five rounds per second—impossibly fast next to the American corollary, the Browning Automatic Rifle or "BAR," which fired at just over ten rounds per second. Joe stared transfixed at the maelstrom for an instant, certain that nothing could withstand the shrieking stream.

As the machine gunner began to lace the ground around them with bursts, everyone fell back, away from the gun, running down the hill or over the nearby ridgeline. Joe found himself with Barney and two other soldiers crammed in a shallow ditch. They appeared to be alone, separated from the rest of the unit by the ridgeline they'd been following. The gun's muzzle flashes had placed it around 200 yards up on the spine of the ridge.

"We have to destroy him."

No one had put Joe in charge, but no one else was talking. Joe was shouting over the gun's din.

"Barney and I can mortar him."

Mortaring without moving seemed much better than advancing on the thing.

"You two go downslope and flank him."

Joe didn't know where he was getting the ideas, but no one was stopping him. The two other soldiers nodded their heads.

"We'll start to mortar him in five minutes. When we've fired ten rounds, open up on the gun from your position and we'll assault through from here."

"Why only ten rounds?" asked one of them.

"That's all we have."

The two men made to bolt down the slope when Joe stopped them.

"We need to synchronize our watches. It's 2:17 on my mark."

The men were bounding away when Joe added, "Don't shoot us."

This time, Joe used the mortar properly. Barney armed the rounds for 200 yards and took a position to spot once the shooting started. Joe adjusted the knobs and windage on the tube to the shadow where they had seen the muzzle flashes. At 2:22, he started his pattern. Barney guided him.

"Twenty short. Two degrees right…"

Joe corrected and kept dropping the rounds in the tube. His last round was just clear of the tube when he grabbed his M-1 and started a zigzag sprint in the direction of the gun. Barney was putting down covering fire from his own M-1 and Joe could hear the reassuring judder of the BAR from his friends' flanking fire. He slid to a stop behind a small hummock and was about to begin his own covering fire when he noticed that the disordered roar around him no longer included the terrifying shriek of the German gun.

Barney stopped shooting and commenced his own zigzag sprint as Joe opened up with his M-1 at the smoky depression in the ridgeline. He had nearly emptied his magazine when a small patch of white fluttered into view in the middle of his sight picture.

Joe was intent on keeping their heads down until he or Barney could get close enough to use a hand grenade. He registered the white flag without registering its meaning and kept pulling the trigger until his spent magazine sprang from his M-1.

The hillside was quiet. The white flag was waving insistently now. Joe put a fresh magazine in his M-1 and chambered a round, before turning to see Barney doing the same thing. Joe motioned Barney to stay still as he stood and started to walk toward the flag, never allowing it to waver far from his front sight. To his left, the two flankers were doing the same.

As Joe drew closer, he was able to take in the scene: a mangled M-42 at the head of a slit trench with two men splayed motionless next to it, and a man in feldgrau waving a handkerchief at the collapsed mouth of a bunker. The man made eye contact and, not being shot, stepped from the bunker with both hands high. Joe was wondering what to do with him when another man emerged from the bunker, then another.

In a moment, Barney had joined Joe and the four of them were aiming their guns at twelve panzergrenadiers crowded into the slit trench with their hands held high. Barney moved his muzzle to indicate they should leave the trench and they did so.

Joe's first thought as the Germans stood before him on the same level was that they were huge, and not just because their hands were held high. Surrendering or not, they stood upright and looked insuperably martial in clean, well-kept gear. Several—in fact almost all of them—were bleeding from their ears. The concussion of Joe's mortars had done its work.

One was clearly in charge. Even with his hands on his bare head, he looked almost relaxed. As he took in his surroundings, Joe could see his surprise at having surrendered his twelve soldiers to four diminutive yellow men. Joe could see something else, too. The bullets in the belt draped over his shoulder had blue tips.

At first, Joe thought they were tracer rounds, but tracers were normally placed into a belt at intervals of several rounds. Firing a belt entirely of burning tracer rounds would scorch out a barrel. Joe was marveling at the man's assurance when he realized what they actually were. The Germans had been known from time to time to use plastic or wooden bullets in their machine guns. The slug splinters were invisible to x-ray, consigning surviving wounded to an agony of uncertain recovery. Why the man chose to surrender with his bandoleer instead of leaving it in his bunker, he would never say, but Joe caught the slightest smirk on his face as he took in his captors.

Concealing thickets from the ravine bottom covered their downhill slope. The four outnumbered Americans had no friends in sight. The German caught Joe's eyes and held them.

Joe was not calculating the risk of their position. He wasn't visualizing the plastic bullets doing their work. He wasn't even remembering the last look of happy relief on Ernie's face. He was simply stepping to the German and bringing his M-1 to his shoulder as the man's eyes widened in recognition of the most horrible miscalculation of his life.

Joe pulled the trigger in the man's face from two feet.

TEXANS

Rhineland Campaign—Vosges Mountains
Bruyères, France
34 Months After Pearl Harbor

I'm so proud of you, Joe. Barely in Europe a month and already you're a staff sergeant. I can picture you with just three of your friends honchoing those eleven Germans off the mountain.

Joe sat at the edge of his freshly dug foxhole in the foothills outside Nice as he started to read Fumi's latest letter. The company commander hadn't explained his promotion, but Joe assumed it had to do with his eliminating the German mortar at Sassetta.

The regiment had bivouacked outside Nice after arriving by ship from Italy at the Port of Marseille. The invasion of southern France had followed the Normandy invasion by a couple of months. Arriving after the Allies had secured Marseille and Toulon, 442 had been posted to the high ground north of Nice.

The unit spent several weeks acculturating to the lushly vegetated hills of Provence, patrolling and mopping up German stragglers who had not joined the rest of OB West under Field Marshall Gunther von Kluge as it fled to its highly defensible redoubt in the Vosges Mountains. The conscripted Eastern Europeans that largely comprised OB West had proven less of a problem than their regular Wehrmacht counterparts in Italy. Joe and his friends expected pursuit warfare, driving the enemy before them on their way to Germany.

It was early fall. The mountain air was crisp. Joe could not stop looking from the arresting azure of the Mediterranean off one shoulder to the snowy peaks of the Maritime Alps off the other.

He was curious for the news from Honolulu, and he was half hoping that Fumi had not freighted him with another adoring description of Dr. Ishii, but he would have to wait to find out.

"Listen up, men."

Joe set aside Fumi's letter as the new platoon leader, Lt. Rich Hanley, stood in the middle of the bivouac with his hands on his hips. The men fell silent and turned to him.

"We have a chore."

Something in his manner gave Joe pause.

"A battalion of Texans has been isolated on a finger ridge outside of the town of Bruyères. They can't break through the Germans around them and they're nearly out of ammo."

Joe knew what was coming. He turned to Barney next to him. "Surrender would seem reasonable."

He thought he'd whispered, but Lt. Hanley obviously heard him. He stopped and turned to face Joe. At least he was smiling.

"My sentiments exactly, Hoochi. We're going up there to persuade them to do just that—the Germans, that is."

Joe wondered why supplies could not be airdropped to the Texans. As if he'd read his thoughts, Lt. Hanley continued.

"The weather at that altitude limits air ops and the drops they've managed have fallen outside the Texans' perimeter."

Lt. Hanley drew the men in around him as he unfolded a map and pointed to their destination, hard against the westernmost border of France with Germany.

"Bruyères is in the Vosges Mountains. You fellows from the Pacific Northwest might find it familiar. It's high, steep, and densely forested."

The deuce-and-a-halfs were at the Company bivouac at 0600 the next morning. Joe wondered at the mass of materiel offloaded at Marseille and Toulon in the few weeks since the Allies had landed. There seemed to be no end of OD green vehicles with stenciled white stars.

Joe also noticed that the unit seemed to get things done faster and with less talking. Even the new replacements for the Italy casualties were lined up at the roadside with their squad mates in the half-light, their gear tied tight for the trip.

They were about to make a lot of mothers in Texas happy—and a lot of quiet women in the camps and across Hawaii sad.

✳   ✳   ✳

Joe missed the suffocating heat of Mississippi.

He'd figured out why the Vosges were so densely forested—it never stopped raining. The wind didn't help, either. Nothing kept out the wet. The rain made its way under his poncho and the muddy trail puddles soaked his pant legs. Joe would later learn that winter warfare in snow was much less miserable than campaigning in the freezing mountain rain of October. There simply was no way to get dry and no way to stay warm, except by moving.

At least they were almost always moving, patrolling the ring of hills around Bruyères to clear the Germans—and their artillery—from the hilltops between them and the stranded Texans. The constant movement to contact in the thick forest was terrifying. They were oblivious to the whereabouts of the enemy until they found themselves in enfilading fire from overlapping MG-42s or mortared from places unseen in the enveloping green.

Worse, they soon discovered that they were not fighting reluctant Russian conscripts. Prisoners proved to be panzergrenadiers—regular Wehrmacht mechanized infantrymen, many hardened in murderous engagements on the Eastern Front.

What really drew their blood, however, were the tree bursts. The Germans appeared to have recorded the coordinates of every draw and every ridge in the trackless forest. They primed the shells from their 88s to detonate in the treetops, showering the troops below in shrapnel and deadly wood splinters.

No one was prepared for the cascade of casualties.

Men digging in for the night wrestled their entrenching tools to scrape shallow foxholes from the rocky, root-riven soil to huddle miserably in the puddled water within, only to realize that they were naked without a covering of logs overhead. Pressing deadfall and nearby saplings into expedient service as a roof was some help.

Joe and Barney never fired their mortar. They couldn't see enough to choose a target. Instead, they patrolled with everyone else, closing to contact and driving the enemy away with small arms and grenades. Two days of patrolling had reduced Joe's twelve-man formation to eight. The ranking NCO, Joe led his team cautiously but steadily, as part of several companies clearing the Western flank of the ridge that held the Texans.

"You guys on flank keep us in sight as we move. I'm the only one with a marked map with coordinates."

The two men charged with securing the patrol's flanks nodded that they understood.

"Hand signals only," Joe added.

They moved slowly through the gloom of the forest understory alert to every sound or movement. The carpet of pine needles silenced their footfalls against the muffled din of the sporadic firefights of their cohorts elsewhere in the thick woods of the mountain. The patrols stayed rigidly within their assigned sectors to avoid engaging each other, but they all moved fast to clear the slopes to the beleaguered Texans.

Joe and Barney were out front with four others loosely arrayed behind them when they heard the distant growl of a big engine. Joe held up his fist to signal a halt. He tried to quiet his labored breathing.

"It sounds like a tank," Barney whispered. "How can it get around up here?"

Joe was shaking his head to indicate that it couldn't possibly be a tank when they both heard the metallic staccato of a tank tread.

"There must be a logging trail up front," he whispered.

Barney shook his head in anguish. "We've got to take him out. He'll kill us all."

Joe turned and motioned to one of the men behind them. Harry Nakano hustled forward with his bazooka and four rockets.

"Harry, there's got to be a logging trail out front. This guy is close or we wouldn't hear him. Set up at trail's edge and take him out. Wait until he's close or you won't kill him and he'll kill us all."

Harry said nothing and headed into the trees. Joe and the rest of the patrol followed at a distance until the logging trail came into view. They lay prone in the pine needles well inside the trees when Harry took a knee behind a large pine at the trail's edge. The engine grew louder. Joe knew that infantry support likely trailed in the woods behind the tank, planning to mop up whatever the tank didn't kill first.

The engine grew steadily louder through the trees. Finally, it sounded close enough to crush them, but still no sign of the tank. Suddenly, it hove into view at a bend in the trail 100 yards out. Joe could not help but admire for a moment the effectiveness of its green and gray camouflage.

The tank closed to sixty yards. Joe knew the flash of Harry's hit would happen now. It didn't. The tank continued steadily forward. Joe's eyes darted to Harry, unmoving behind his tree, and back at the tank, now a mere fifty yards out and looming impossibly larger with every second. Still no shot. Joe suddenly worried that Harry had frozen.

The tank was only twenty yards out and Joe was about to yell at Harry when he heard a low pneumatic rush and saw the fiery exhaust from the rear of Harry's bazooka tube. The front of the tank disappeared in a blinding white flash.

The blast slapped Joe across his whole body. He lay on the pine needles listening to the secondary explosions within the tank as flames and black smoke boiled out of the hole Harry had made in it.

After a moment, the scene before him registered. Harry lay against the trunk of another tree in an awkward, broken attitude. He was still, his face frozen in a rictus of concrete concentration. The trees beyond the tank began to sparkle with muzzle flashes as Joe recognized the churning rip of German machine guns and saw the trees above him receiving the rounds in small eruptions of bark and splinters. After a moment, the hollow cough of mortar tubes joined the chorus. The mortar rounds began exploding in the dense pine canopy behind them, tearing great holes in the almost solid mass and scoring the earth underneath with hammer blows of superheated, supersonic steel and wood.

"Up, goddammit. Assault through! We die if we stay here. They'll walk those mortars onto us."

Joe was on his feet as he yelled, shouldering his M-1 as he ran, pulling the trigger as fast as he could and sweeping the barrel before him. Barney and the others were spread out over twenty yards to either side of him doing the same thing, The reassuring judder of his right flank's BAR—guttural, almost subterranean— seemed somehow more solid, more decisive than the high-pitched shriek of the enemies' weapons. Joe watched almost absently as a large bush danced under the impact of the BAR's slugs until he saw the two men with the MG-42 underneath shuddering lifelessly in the .30 caliber hail.

Joe's ammunition clip pinged out of the M-1's breech with a high musical note and Joe realized, as he pressed home its fresh replacement, that no one seemed to be shooting at them any longer. But the Texans would keep dying above them until Joe and his friends reached them.

"Keep going. Push them straight up the hill into the Texans."

The men slowed to a deliberate walk, moving from tree to tree in a rough skirmish line and training their weapons on the slope above them. Joe guessed they were less than 100 yards from the tabletop of the ridge when the distinctive bark of a BAR came from above them. Joe raised his fist and took a knee behind a tree. The rest of the men did so, as well.

He had not yet spoken when a German stepped from behind a tree twenty yards in front of them. Joe and two others shot him before anyone registered his white handkerchief. Barney spoke.

"That's a BAR up there."

"We don't know who's shooting it," countered Joe.

"Well, the guys we're relieving are supposed to be up on the tabletop where that gun is," Barney insisted. "Do you want to kill them after losing our guys to save them?"

Joe shared Barney's concern, but he did not want to lead his patrol into a trap.

"Kamerad!"

The scream came from deeper in the trees. Joe and Barney stared at each other until the plea was repeated – louder.

Joe turned to both sides of his team. "I think they're boxed between us and the Texans uphill. I'm calling them out, but be ready in case it's a trick."

Joe couldn't remember if he still had a full clip. He replaced it before calling one of his few words of German.

"*Raus*! Get out!"

Two hands, palms facing them, emerged from behind the same tree. Joe thought he could see them shaking.

"Raus, goddamnit," he snarled, louder.

A soldier emerged from behind the tree in a camouflage smock and abbreviated paratroop helmet. Joe had heard the better units had been issued new gear. Hands high above his head, the German faced Joe. Joe did nothing and, after a moment, the German barked something over his shoulder.

The underbrush began to rustle and men began to step out from it. One, then two, from directly behind the first, and then, when no one opened fire, the whole slope seemed to come alive with surrendering Germans. After a few moments, nearly a platoon's worth stood in a nervous knot of upraised hands facing seven equally apprehensive Americans. Joe made a palm down hand gesture to indicate that no one should move. He turned to his men.

"Any one of them so much as sneezes, you take them all out."

Then he cupped his hands and shouted uphill.

"Advance and be recognized."

Silence.

He tried again.

"We're 442. Tell us who you are."

After a moment, a quieter response.

"You the Japs?"

Joe and Barney exchanged glances. Joe suddenly felt a little less worried about the identity of his unseen interlocutor. He took a moment to answer.

"No. We're the Americans that look like Japs."

"What's the call sign?"

Joe did not have an answer. They'd been out of contact and without a radio throughout their patrol and the only call sign he knew—"Easy," countersign "Money"—was two days out of date.

"We don't have the current one."

Silence.

Barney spoke quietly. Growing confidence notwithstanding, they'd been warned repeatedly about clever, English-speaking Germans masquerading as Americans.

"We push the prisoners to them. We cover them from behind and wait to see how the guys up there receive them."

Joe had no better idea. He shouted uphill again.

"We've got prisoners down here. We're going to push them to you. Anyone makes a wrong move and we shoot them from behind and mortar your position."

After a pause, "Gee, thanks."

They climbed very deliberately for several minutes with Joe periodically calling out to show their position while the rest of his men covered their prisoners nervously. Joe nearly missed the first friendly position—a BAR barely protruding from a brush pile at the base of a tree. The brush parted to reveal a bearded, hollow-eyed man in fatigues greasy with other men's blood. He stood slowly, staring slack-jawed at Joe. He said nothing. Joe realized the man's cheeks were wet. Joe stepped to him and pulled a pack of Luckies from his fatigues. The man just stood there. Finally, Joe lit a cigarette and handed it to him. At this, two others emerged from under the brush.

The German prisoners, well fed and relatively clean, stood in a nervous knot staring at the filthy, cadaverous soldiers who had resisted them for a week and now held them captive.

Other Americans began to emerge from their fighting positions and Joe realized as he looked around that he was surrounded by the detritus of shattered trees and men.

The soldier before Joe had yet to say anything and his cigarette smoldered unsmoked in his hand. Joe was about to walk on when his new friend grabbed his forearm with both hands, surprising him with the strength of his grip.

"Every one of us was a dead man."

*   *   *

Three hours later, Joe stood before the aid station at the bottom of the hill after carrying in a wounded Texan. Beneath a collection of tarps strung between trees at the trailside, doctors and medics moved constantly between prostrate men, cutting off clothes, cleaning and dressing wounds, repairing the damage. The noise of the wounded was punctuated by instructions between those attending them, quiet, but still clear above the babble.

Stretchers lined the uphill side of the trail. Medics moved constantly among them, hovering over some with morphine and sulfa while dispensing with others after a moment's observation. Joe's eyes were drawn to the downhill side of the trail. Lined up shoulder to shoulder were figures wrapped in ponchos. Joe chided himself for thinking they resembled rubberized egg rolls. From each figure, a pair of muddy boots protruded onto the grass at the trail's edge. Joe started to walk the rank of boots, a prone parade rest stretching off into the late afternoon shadows of the forest.

Pale and insistent among the file of boots, a single naked foot shone. Joe stopped before it. After a moment, he took a knee. He resolved to make the sign of the cross and move on, but instead, he crossed himself and reached up to pull back the edge of the poncho covering the face underneath.

Franny looked like he was about to laugh.

*　　*　　*

Joe and nearly everyone else had collapsed into a narcotic sleep almost immediately after coming off the mountain. Division had billeted the regiment in the buildings around Bruyères. Early the next morning, the smell of bacon, eggs, and coffee drew Joe from his field expedient cocoon of GI wool blanket and poncho and out into the predawn mountain chill. The cooks had prepared breakfast in the town square.

Bacon had never been part of a Japanese breakfast—smoked fish and musubi rice with a raw egg mixed in was customary— but the signature breakfast meat had quickly become one of the first American customs to be embraced by the new arrivals. In the words of Bing Crosby, "There's nothing bacon doesn't make better."

Joe would feel ashamed later, but as he blinked himself awake and pulled on his boots without tying them, he could think of nothing but the meal waiting outside.

The town square was a mass of soldiers queuing up in the predawn darkness. The cooks knew their business and Joe stood with a steaming mess tin of bacon, eggs, and grits and his canteen cup full of coffee before he had time to complain about having to wait. He inhaled the food and the scalding coffee before he remembered that he had to find Sparky or Harry.

The crowd of soldiers in the low light precluded his recognizing anyone from Bravo Company. He was about to find a place to relieve himself when Sparky spoke from behind.

"Joe."

The tone of Sparky's voice told Joe that he already knew. Joe turned around to find Sparky standing listlessly and struggling to meet his eyes. Joe couldn't speak, so he just nodded his head, sparing Sparky the burden of articulating the news. The two of them just stood there until Sparky finally straightened up.

"I was there," he said. "He was pulling flank security while the rest of the squad assaulted a machine gun position."

Joe pictured Franny thoughtfully selecting a place of concealment among the tangled forest.

"A German patrol overran him."

Joe pictured Franny crouched behind a tree, alone, frantically emptying his M-1 at unnumbered attackers.

"He held them off until we took out the gun."

Joe closed his eyes, hoping he would better control his breathing.

"We found four dead Germans in front of his hidey hole."

Joe had never associated Franny with lethality. Then again, he'd never associated himself with tears.

"Two of them had died by bayonet."

Joe couldn't help himself. He didn't care if he was sobbing in heaves. He saw in his mind's eye little Franny who was always laughing, out of ammo and stepping from his concealment to defend his friends with all he had left—steel.

"The LT has put him in for a Silver Star."

*   *   *

It was another week before Division pulled 442 out of the line. The very afternoon after breakfast in Bruyères, they were back in the mountains harrying the Germans from the sector with constant movement to contact, driving the Germans before them with envelopments and enfilades. Air strikes had limited utility once they'd discovered that the smoke they popped to mark their own positions under the green canopy could just as easily be seen by the German artillery spotters. A serial refrain of bullets, Bouncing Betties, and tree bursts—and continuing casualties.

Through it all, the inescapable wet and cold. Sodden at best and often soaked in the cold wind, their only rest came in sporadic halts. Fires were out of the question. Sleep was fitful naps shivering in the water gathered in the hollows of their shallow fighting holes until they were too tired not to sleep anyway.

Few mothers could have recognized their sons among the gaunt, hollow-eyed apparitions shambling slowly down the trails to Bruyères after the sector had been declared secure.

Joe and Barney were falling from one foot to the other, too tired to look up at the town below them, passing Reggie Sakamoto's rucksack between them. He'd been carried off the mountain two days earlier after tripping a mine. For all they knew, they were humping the ruck of a dead man.

Had they not spent their whole lives in the islands, they would have recognized an incipient first snowfall in the air. But for going downhill, neither one could have continued walking. Joe adopted a kind of suspended awareness, concentrating on the rest below rather than on the torment of getting to it. Hot coffee and food, a smoke, a dry place to sleep… After two hours, Joe turned a corner in the trail and it hit him full in the face: the overpowering invitation of bacon and coffee on the wind. Bruyères was no longer below them. He could see it in front of them through the trees, not three hundred yards off.

Without meaning to, both Barney and Joe picked up their pace. Moments later, they were stepping from the trees on the town's edge on a beeline to the town square, the source of the siren scent.

Joe did not care for the expression on Lieutenant Hanley's face when he noticed him standing next to the first building.

"Men, we have a formation on the soccer field on the west side of town at 1000 Hours."

It was 0945 Hours.

Lieutenant Hanley read their faces.

"They're calling it 'The Rescue of the Lost Battalion.' A reporter from *Star and Stripes* has come up to do a story on it and the commanding general wants a pass in review."

Without breaking stride, Joe and Barney turned away from the bacon with an effort not unlike lifting a too-heavy barbell.

Troops gathering in formation are normally alive with movement—noncoms marshalling their soldiers into position, lieutenants squaring up the platoons, captains aligning their companies—all with commands barked crisply across the assembly. This was different. The men moved slowly. Commands were low, almost muttered. At 0955 hours, the ranks were dressed and the season's first snow had started to fall. The men stood at parade rest, shivering in the wind.

1000 Hours came and went. No general.

The minutes passed. Men started to shiver more violently. The regimental commander stood facing his men, his face growing darker. No one said a word.

It was nearly 1100 hours and Colonel Miller was about to dismiss his troops when the commanding general's shiny sedan glided to a halt behind him.

Colonel Miller had been the assistant regimental commander. He had taken command two weeks earlier when Colonel Pence, his predecessor, had become a casualty. The Army would award Colonel Miller the Silver Star for having repeatedly, in the face of withering fire, rallied his men and directed their movements during the rescue.

Now the driver dismounted and ran to open the general's door. The general stepped from his sedan. The regimental sergeant major called the ranks to attention. Colonel Miller spun on his heel and braced his entire being into a crisp salute. He spoke in a flat parade cadence.

"442nd Regimental Combat Team all present or accounted for, sir."

The general didn't return the salute. Instead, he stopped and put his hands on his hips. His subordinate held his salute as the general slowly panned the dressed ranks of drawn, filthy, shivering men behind him. The only things that shone were their weapons at port arms and the red, white and blue of the flags at the head of the formation.

The general's face hardened as he finally looked directly at the colonel. He didn't wait to address his subordinate later. He didn't step closer to speak quietly out of earshot of his subordinate's men. He stayed where he was and kept his hands on his hips as he raised his chin to announce.

"Colonel, when I told you to assemble the regiment, I meant the entire regiment."

The general was displeased at the small size of the formation because he did not know that nearly 800 men of his command had become casualties rescuing 200 Texans.

Colonel Miller held his salute in silence. As the seconds passed, the general's face began to fall. When Colonel Miller had finally gathered enough breath, his voice was choked and uneven, but his low growl carried over the entire parade.

"Sir, this is the entire regiment."

UNFRIENDLY FIRE

Rhineland Campaign—Maritime Alps
Nice, France
36 Months After Pearl Harbor

Joe, you know I'm proud of you. I worry about you. I care about you.

Not a bad beginning, Joe thought to himself. Fumi's letter had arrived in a backlog of mail at the regiment's winter defensive position in the Maritime Alps above Nice. Joe's squad occupied a well-made German bunker, dry and warmed by a liberated pot-bellied stove. The bunker's entrance gave onto a sky scape of snow-covered peaks stretching to the horizon. The crags in the midday sun were the brightest white Joe had ever seen.

Every day, replacements arrived to fill the places of those lost in the Vosges. They were folded into the generally uneventful, preventive patrols in the surrounding mountains – strenuous ascents in a picture postcard of powder snow.

Joe did not want to leave.

Now he settled into his liberated rocking chair and poured a cup of coffee from the fresh pot on the stove. He hadn't heard from Fumi in weeks and wanted to savor her feelings for him.

A Lucky was the perfect complement to the surprisingly good Army coffee. He held his first draw in his lungs, prolonging the velvet sting of the rich smoke.

I know we mean a lot to each other, but I've never been clear that we're an item.

This made Joe wonder if he should start to compile an inventory of the things he didn't like about Fumi. Nothing came to mind, so he kept reading.

But I think you should know that James—Dr. Ishii—and I have come to mean a lot to each other.

Joe put down his cup of coffee.

A natural consequence, I guess, of watching someone, day in and day out, dispel despair with hope.

Spare me the Barnard histrionics, Joe thought. He forgot to draw on his cigarette and kept reading.

In any case, we've decided to marry.

"What the fuck?" he breathed aloud. "How long has she known this living saint?"

"What living saint?"

Sparky and Harry were standing in the entry, backlit by the brilliance of the sunlit snow on the mountains behind them. Joe looked up and said nothing, but dropped the letter to the floor.

"A letter from Fumi?" Sparky asked.

Joe just shook his head.

"Come on," Sparky said. "We're going to Maman's. You too, Barney."

Barney was the only other person in the room. He brightened at this. *Maman*, French for mother, was a widow who served home-cooked meals in her old farmhouse halfway down the mountain. Colonel Miller had told her she could serve officers only if no enlisted soldiers needed the space.

Joe still said nothing, so Sparky stepped in and pulled him upright.

"Barney. Grab his coat."

Half an hour later, the four of them sat on benches at a plank table in a room lit by kerosene lamps and warmed by a fire in a river stone hearth. The room was crowded with other soldiers and the aroma of several plump chickens roasting in a large cast iron stove. Just the smell of the place made it worth visiting. Maman put a bottle of red wine and four well used glasses on the table.

"Did Fumi break it off – whatever it was?" Sparky asked.

Joe's first swallow of wine improved his mood. Maman's wine was produced nearby and bottled in whatever presented, but it would have tasted great even to men not starved for good food and drink.

"She's marrying a doctor from Tripler."

Sparky nodded while Harry and Barney concentrated on their wine.

"What did you expect, Joe? You left without even asking her to wait."

Joe nodded.

"You can't blame her, Joe," Harry said.

Joe still said nothing, so Harry continued.

"We all like her. She's a great girl."

Joe raised his eyebrows. "Is that supposed to help, Harry?"

"No one wants you to feel bad, Joe," Sparky intervened. "We just don't want to bad mouth Fumi."

"He's taking advantage of a fighting man in harm's way," Joe said. His tone—equal parts wounded, yet brave—made the other three smile.

Joe had finished his first glass of wine. The smallest sip filled his whole head with a taste he really liked. He was starting to feel unaccountably better about the world. He even started to smile.

"You might consider counselling?" Sparky offered. He was referring to recent news that a prominent psychologist had propounded "counselling" to repair soldiers' emotional wounds—to the derision of most soldiers.

Joe was pouring his second glass and saw Sparky's joke for the opening it was.

"Do you think anyone would pay for my advice?" he asked.

*   *   *

Joe was glad his squad had no assigned patrol the next day. He awoke at first light with a splitting headache in unhappy vindication of his boyhood catechism, which had promised punishment for misconduct. Coffee, a smoke, and a shower largely returned him to life. Breakfast was in order.

A garrison breakfast was Joe's favorite part of the Army. Good food and coffee in quantity. He was trying to decide between bacon and ham with his fried eggs when he saw the notice tacked to one of the poles supporting the large chow tent: "Catholic Mass at 1100 Hrs."

The regiment's chaplain was Episcopalian—nice enough, but not ideal for a Catholic. Division had never sent a Catholic priest before, so Joe decided he would attend.

Mass in the mountains, held in the open air on a greensward next to the motor pool, was different for Joe, but still familiar. The old rhythms were unchanged, and Joe found himself back in tiny Damien Church at Kamalo, kneeling and standing to the priest's prayers, repeating the liturgy. He was home. Mass didn't make him homesick. Rather, he found that his headache was gone.

He even paid attention to the homily. Chaplain Curtin was in his forties, Irish from the Bronx. He explained how the Church had chronicled the march of the faith, especially its trials. He described studying in seminary the episodic persecution of Christians throughout the ages. Each wave had produced martyrs—Christians who had decided to die for their faith—and each wave had been assessed on a particular metric, the *ratio edendi*, the ratio of Christians persecuted to those who chose in response to be martyrs. The Chaplain recounted being told he would be visiting 442 and remembering that the *ratio edendi* that most skewed to martyrs—by a dramatic margin— had belonged to the Japanese martyrs. Tens of thousands of Japanese Catholics—16th and 17th-century inheritors of the early Portuguese Jesuit missionaries—had quietly chosen to die rather than deny their faith.

Joe left Mass reluctantly. Chaplain Curtin had set up a field confessional in the woods at the edge of the unit area – a poncho hung between two trees, with a chair on either side of it. The priest took the chair on the other side of the poncho as men lined up for their turn at the sacrament.

Joe found himself at the end of the line. As he stood in the winter air, he appreciated his issue greatcoat. He'd never seen a garment like this before getting to Europe—OD green wool, heavy and stiff at first. Until now, he'd worn it mainly on patrols, constantly moving and even sweating sometimes with his exertions. Now, though, he remembered that it kept off the cold even as he stood still.

The line took longer than he expected as soldiers unburdened themselves. There were comparatively few Nisei Catholic, but a number of non-Catholics had seized the opportunity to talk to someone. He finally took his seat after waiting for forty minutes.

The priest had an easy manner. 442 was not his first line assignment. In fact, line assignments were all he'd done for the last two years.

"Bless me Father for I have sinned," Joe began. "It's been…"

Joe paused, trying to remember his last confession.

"Don't worry," the priest said. "An honest guess is fine."

"I'm pretty sure I haven't confessed since I was a teenager, Father."

"That's fine. You're here now, soldier."

"Father, I can't remember most of my sins."

"An honest estimate is fine."

"Well, I've done all the expected ones—greed, pride, lying, impatience, lack of charity… Nothing that really sticks out."

"Is that it?"

Another pause, but shorter.

"Well, of course, there's women," Joe said.

He felt a little foolish as he said it. There had not been many women and they had not included the one he really wanted.

"Are you married, soldier?"

"No, Father."

"That's important. Have any of the women been married?"

No pause this time – the list was short.

"No, Father."

"Are you sorry for what you did with them?"

Joe had forgotten about this part of confession. He wasn't sorry. In fact, he wished there'd been more. So he said nothing.

After an uncomfortable pause, the priest exhaled noisily.

"Look, soldier. This isn't a test. God wants you to have absolution and no one expects you to be a choir boy."

"No, Father."

"Are you disagreeing with me?"

"No, Father. I meant I'm not a choir boy."

"But you have to be sorry for what you've done to receive absolution."

"Father, I don't want to lie to you. I don't feel particularly sorry about that one."

"You do realize it's a mortal sin?"

"I do."

"So you realize it offends God?"

"Well… It's almost all I think about."

It was the priest's turn to pause. Finally, he spoke.

"You're a soldier at war and my mission is to prepare you for the worst. Do you follow me?"

"Of course, Father."

Joe added before the priest could respond, "That's why I can't lie to you, Father. Not at a time like this."

At this, the priest was silent for a while. Finally, Joe could hear him shift in his field chair and lean in closer to the intervening poncho.

"God made women beautiful and endlessly intriguing. We're supposed to want them."

Joe stopped himself from saying, "Thank God." He was somewhat encouraged, though, by the priest's choice of the plural subject.

"Yes, Father."

"You're not made of stone."

"Yes, Father."

"You don't need to say yes to my every sentence."

"Yes, Father."

At this, the priest took a rest. Joe thought he could hear him rubbing his head.

"All that is needed is for you to acknowledge the wrongness of your acts and to be sorry for them," he said finally.

It was Joe's turn to pause. Finally, he answered.

"Father, if you're asking me will it ever happen again, I've got to tell you the chances are pretty good."

Joe thought he might have heard the priest laugh.

"Look, soldier. God doesn't require a theology colloquy. You are a soldier in one of the hardest fighting units of the European Theater—of any theater, actually. God loves you for the sacrifices you've made, and for the ones you're going to make."

Joe could not disagree, so the priest went on.

"Do you agree that women are God's children, deserving of your love, protection, and respect?"

Joe refrained from remarking on a descending order of magnitude and simply said, "Yes."

"You are absolved."

As he crossed himself to leave, Joe was suddenly, unbidden, staring again into the horrified eyes of the German NCO in his last moments.

He hadn't really thought about it since doing it, but he suddenly found himself wondering if the man had kids. He pictured little blond children smiling up at their soldier father. He could hear the priest getting out of his chair and decided to leave nothing unsaid.

"There might be something else, Father."

He could hear the chair settle again.

"Yes, Soldier?"

"I killed a man."

"A German?"

"Yes."

"That's why you're here."

"He was unarmed. He'd surrendered."

The priest had heard this before—a lot. He had entered the clergy later in life after several years as an Assistant Manhattan DA. He understood extenuation.

Joe was opening his mouth to speak when the priest added, "Don't leave anything out."

Joe nodded even though the priest could not see him and began. "We had lost a guy subduing a German machine gun bunker. There were four of us. We were in an isolated draw – not within easy support from any friendlies. We saw a white flag and expected two or three prisoners, but twelve of them came out. The ranking NCO worried me, so I shot him."

Joe was out of breath when he finished.

The priest waited a moment before asking, "How did you shoot him?"

"I walked up to him and shot him in the face with my M-1."

"Why?"

"Father, I didn't really think about it. They looked surprised there were so few of us. We had no support nearby. And the NCO was smirking."

"So you shot him because he was smirking?"

"I shot him because they outnumbered us three to one and he didn't look scared enough not to jump us."

The priest said nothing.

"He also had a bandoleer of plastic bullets."

The priest knew what that meant. They both sat in silence for a moment.

"Honestly, I hadn't thought about it until now," Joe said. "I was our senior leader and I acted to remove the risk."

At this, the priest cross examined.

"So why mention the smirk and the plastic bullets?"

"Because you said to leave nothing out."

The priest was quiet for a minute, then asked, "Put aside the smirk and the bullets. Did they present a risk to you and your men?"

Joe didn't hesitate. "I thought they did, and I still do."

After a moment, he added, "The look on his face and his plastic bullets just made it easier."

There was no more to say, so Joe waited. After a few moments, the decision came down.

"I'm not giving you absolution for shooting him."

Joe felt a slight spasm of alarm.

"Because you committed no sin in doing so."

Joe would have felt more relieved if he'd ever felt guilty about it, but he was glad for the confirmation that God felt the same way.

The priest took a moment to compose his explanation.

"Moral ambiguity is one of the cruelest wounds of war. Soldiers have to make awful decisions in an instant and then live with them. Imagine the gunner who takes out a church full of people because of the sniper in the steeple. He didn't put him there, but he has to protect his comrades. So did you," the priest said. "God doesn't require you to parse your decisions afterwards when you have a split second to act in defense of your friends. The fact that the German was smirking and carrying plastic bullets only made your decision easier. It didn't make it wrong. God loves you and gives you the benefit of the doubt."

*   *   *

Confession is supposed to be secret, but Joe's was overheard. Ten yards away from Joe and Father Curtin, one of the newest replacements hovered, hidden in the trees, over his personal slit trench. Major Kenji "Kenneth" Kimura was a career Adjutant General Corps officer who had just arrived from commanding the rear detachment in Honolulu. He replaced the regimental Executive Officer killed in the Vosges. Major Kimura was a trim man, some would say prim, even. He didn't care to use a latrine soiled by other men, so he had dug his own.

The lead story in the latest *Stars and Stripes*, "Nisei Rescue Lost Battalion," promised growing prominence for the men fortunate enough to survive Europe. As he settled in for a leisurely read, Kimura realized someone was hearing Catholic confessions nearby, and he could overhear them. He found the confessions ordinary, typical of men unable to take the long or the sophisticated view. The last one, though, stood him abruptly upright. He craned to identify the penitent soldier as he left.

*   *   *

Pibales are glass eels, tiny translucent baby eels harvested in Mediterranean estuaries after their parents mate in the middle of the Atlantic's Sargasso Sea. Delicious deep-fried in olive oil and dusted with cider vinegar and sea salt like French fries, but more nourishing and expensive, the waterfront eateries of Nice routinely served them in paper cones. Joe and his friends had ordered them.

Joe enjoyed duty above Nice. The scenery was spectacular and Nice itself was only an hour away on one of the Army transports constantly moving between the port city and the mountain garrisons. Winter in Nice was like spring almost everywhere else, with bright, crisp days and chilly nights—a garden next to the mud, sleet, and snow of the Vosges. The city itself had been a leisure destination for prominent Europeans and combined grand boulevards and buildings with pebbly beaches on the uniquely blue Mediterranean. Joe couldn't stop wondering how Fumi would've enjoyed seeing it, too. He could just picture her lighting up at the impressionist pastels of the seascape before him, her eyes nearly black, but somehow bright.

La Colombe, The Dove, was a standard eatery at the water's edge. Its picture windows gave onto a pristine beach with brightly painted fishing boats on the inshore scree. You could almost ignore the smudge of smoky gray transports and warships further off at the port. Half of the patrons were locals, well fed and well dressed. Joe wondered if they had collaborated to survive so well the previous occupiers.

Joe, Sparky and Harry were eating pibales and drinking cold beer while waiting for their main course. Nice's local fishing fleet had forestalled the privation that stalked most of Europe and grilled lobster was on offer for a very modest amount of military scrip. The men were discussing the balance of their European war, and Harry was optimistic.

"We've run the Germans out of France. The Russians are romping across Middle Europe."

"The Germans still have one million armed men beyond the Apennines," Sparky cautioned.

Field Marshal Kesselring had erected a string of strong points on the Apennine peaks spanning the northern width of Italy. These had withstood months of Allied assaults. They were called the Gothic Line.

"Between our guys and the Russians," countered Harry, "we'll take Berlin before long. Then the game is over for the Germans in Italy."

"Those guys have the whole Po Valley, from the Apennines to the Alps, to themselves," said Sparky. "They can hold out and as long as they do, they're at least a bargaining chip." He shook his head. "Meanwhile, a straight cost-benefit analysis of our campaigns to date is not encouraging."

"We just took nearly 800 casualties to rescue 200 Texans," Joe added.

"Are you saying we shouldn't have?" Harry recoiled as he spoke.

Sparky shook his head. "No. I think we'd all do it over again."

Joe wasn't entirely sure he would.

"Anyway, what's your point, Spark?" Joe asked.

"My point is just that we need to be ready for more hard duty."

Harry was looking from one to the other. "We all know that, Spark," he said. "Your real point is that we take the hits so our kids never get treated the way we've been treated."

Sparky nodded. "That's right."

Joe motioned to a passing waiter as he held up his nearly empty beer. "*Trois, s'il vous plaît.*"

Joe liked speaking in French. The vowel sounds were nearly the same as those in Japanese and he'd found he sounded almost fluent in short exchanges.

The fresh beers arrived with the three lobsters, glistening red and steaming on their plates with ramekins of melted butter and sliced lemons. The boys went to work. A sharp incision along the underside of each tail enabled easy removal of the succulent white meat within. Joe was chewing happily when he heard his name spoken flatly behind him.

He turned to find two MPs standing too close to the table with their hands on their hips.

"We're taking you back to Regimental HQ."

Joe was about to ask why, but their faces told him there was no point. He looked at the still steaming sea creature before him and shoveled what remained of the tail meat into his mouth. As he stood from the table, Sparky and Harry did the same.

"We only have orders for him," one of the MPs said.

Harry pulled a too large wad of scrip from his pocket and tossed it to the table.

"We could use the ride," he said simply.

The ride up into the mountains was longer and no one felt like talking in front of the MPs as the three of them sat crammed into the rear bench of the small Jeep.

Joe wondered at the reason for his summons and couldn't think of anything he'd done wrong. The last few weeks had been good duty, working in the replacements on hard mountain movements without freezing or fear of imminent death. The replacements had proven adaptable—happy to be part of a unit with burgeoning acclaim. "Proud of the patch," as Harry put it.

Since her last letter, Joe had tried not to think of Fumi, but had generally failed.

A number of the guys had fallen into arrangements with local women who fed them... and more. Not quite commercial, but nakedly expedient friendships. Joe hadn't. The idea just didn't square with his image of himself as a man whose charm was enough. He remained a rake, but Fumi had left him a lonely one.

Could he have done anything differently? He hadn't seen that he could ask her to wait. They were really no more than an interrupted crush. But she was the only crush he had, and her warmth had been a constant comfort. Was she already married? Was she screwing the doctor? Joe told himself she was still a traditional Japanese girl, New York sophisticate or no. He was still wrestling with the question when the MPs led him, alone, into Major Kimura's office.

The room was spare—some maps on the walls, a telephone, and tidy papers on the desk. Joe had never seen the major up close. Now, the man's hands—delicate with perfect pink fingernails—were the only thing Joe could see as they rustled papers. Joe stood at attention before his desk and snapped into a salute. The major didn't look up. Joe held his salute and waited for the reproach that must be coming—his area was sloppy, his gear unorganized. Finally, the major put down his papers and looked up.

"You want to cut throats, don't you?"

Joe was taken aback. What the hell was he talking about?

"Why else would you carry that ridiculous sword in your ruck?"

Joe didn't know what to say, so the major continued.

"I'm preferring you for a general courts-martial on a charge of murder."

Joe felt like he was outside the room, peering in on the victim of some terrible misunderstanding.

"We don't shoot prisoners in the 442," the major continued.

Joe was tempted to say that you need to take a prisoner before you can shoot him. His mind raced. *How the hell could this asshole know? Who the fuck told?*

"If we don't punish misconduct," said the major with a thin smile, "I've got to say the chances are pretty good it will happen again."

*   *   *

"The regimental XO has assigned himself to prosecute you and he's deputed me to be your defense counsel."

LT Hanley sat at his desk in the platoon HQ. Joe, Sparky, and Barney sat on packing crates.

"Uh… are you a lawyer, sir?" Joe asked LT Hanley.

"I'm a stockbroker. It's the same difference."

Barney broke in.

"This is bullshit, sir. That German was ready to have his guys jump us."

LT Hanley nodded. "Then that's our defense."

Barney was more agitated than Joe.

"I'll testify to it, sir," he added.

Sparky compressed his features in disbelief.

"They want to send Joe to Leavenworth?" he asked.

LT Hanley spread his hands. "Murder is a death penalty offense."

The room was silent before Sparky exploded.

"In what universe is this not crazy, sir?"

LT Hanley nodded his head. "You're right, Spark, but you know it's not my call."

"Well, whose is it?" Sparky asked, although everyone knew the answer.

LT Hanley was looking at Joe. "I'll go to Colonel Miller, but the XO is in the general's HQ all the time. He manages admin for the whole unit and Division has come to depend on him. If he says we need to make an example, the general is going to listen."

Joe remembered the pass in review after the rescue of the Texans. He was taking a mental inventory of the unit's officers for assignment to the panel, the military jury. Most of them were good guys. He couldn't see even one of them siding with the XO.

"Sir, I can't see any of our officers voting to convict."

LT Hanley shook his head.

"This is a general court, Joe," he said. "The members are drawn from the entire division."

Joe had kept the enormity of his calamity at bay, insistent that sanity would eventually intrude on the absurd sequence of events. As the conversation continued, Joe was concentrating on his boots, wondering if he'd applied enough grease to keep out the winter wet.

He dimly remembered Mr. Alton discussing a Bohemian writer named Kafka who depicted life as absurd. His stories never seemed to end well. For weeks the guys had heard rumors of an imminent German surrender. No one talked about the Pacific War. Rotation back to Hawaii was the obvious next step. Now LT Hanley took a page from the obscure Bohemian pessimist.

"At any rate, the trial won't happen for a while," he said. "We're shipping back to Italy."

*　　*　　*

Nice, France as a debarkation port was less appealing than Nice as a scenic destination.

442 had spent the previous week staging for the sealift back to Northern Italy—palletizing gear, cleaning weapons, and road marching. Command knew the coming weeks would feature mountain fighting, wresting the Germans from their last mountain fastness. Nearly every day, columns of men crowded the verges of the road between Nice and the unit's mountaintop bivouac. Fifty-pound packs and a punishing grade exhausted them in whichever direction they walked. Joe became reacquainted with the base plate of his mortar as it bruised his shoulders with every footfall.

Now, the idling trucks against the pier fouled the air with diesel fumes, nearly enough to cover the smell of dead fish. Joe and the rest of the regiment waited on the pier in formation for the word to board an old steamer that smelled worse than the pier. The last week's marches had flayed his body but left his mind free to wander. He wished they hadn't.

His impending courts-martial—forestalled, but not rescinded by the movement—filled his thoughts. His initial anger and incredulity had dissipated as the potential consequences took their place at the front of his mind. Execution was simply too awful to contemplate, but prison no longer seemed so absurd. Father Curtin may have absolved him, but Joe began to consider the possibility that his own Army could actually lock him away for absolutely no good reason. He began to assail himself with questions that had no answers.

What if I hadn't shot the German?

Would he have meekly marshalled his men for the march down the mountain?

Or was he just waiting for his moment?

Would he have picked up a rock in an unguarded moment or produced a knife he'd managed to hide?

Maybe the smirk was just a show to reassure his own guys?

Or maybe it was just a nervous tic?

Joe knew the questions were pointless, that they were only making him miserable, but he couldn't stop them. Rather, he replaced them with ones that were worse.

Did the guy have a family?

What did they look like?

This was the worst. Joe could just picture two little blond kids smiling adoringly up at their father. This image would be interrupted by the memory of the pink cloud exploding from the back of the man's head.

Eventually, Joe would manage to return the event to its proper context: a ranking NCO isolated, outnumbered and afraid for his men and himself. Father Curtin had been right and Joe had always known this. His relief, however, would quickly be replaced with thoughts of Fumi.

They weren't even an item, but he'd always assumed they would be.

He hadn't asked her to wait, but he'd never really questioned that she would.

He'd grown accustomed to her constant letters, but he'd never realized how much they meant to him until they stopped.

The letters meant that a beautiful woman on the other side of the planet was thinking about him, was worried about him, was missing him, and wanted him back. He'd never taken the time actually to recognize this, but now he realized it had helped to sustain him through discomfort, fear, sadness...

For the first time in his life, Joe was moody, and his friends noticed.

"Cheer up, brah," Harry said, falling in behind him as the men began to march up the companionway onto the ship.

"What the fuck for, Harry? I've pulled the perfect trifecta of shit. My girl dumps me. The army has decided to execute me for killing a German. But first, I've got to go back to dislodge the only remaining Germans on the planet who've refused to surrender."

"Stop it, brah." Harry braced him.

Joe just shook his head, so Harry continued.

"Stop feeling sorry for yourself. Think about Franny."

Joe raised his chin at this.

"Joe," Harry said, "like it or not, you're a leader now. You can't let the guys see you like this."

Almost imperceptibly, Joe squared his shoulders. Harry smiled.

"Sanity will prevail, brah. They're not going to punish you for protecting your guys. Kimura is just an ambitious fuck kissing up to the commanding general at your expense."

They had made the deck of the old steamer and they both propped their rucks and rifles by the railing and looked out over the harbor. The air up here was fresh with a slight salt breeze blowing in off the water.

Harry pulled a pack of Camels from his breast pocket and offered Joe one. He lit both their cigarettes, and they took in the progressive blue of the water and the sky in the late afternoon sun. The smoke had a sweet edge as Joe drew it deep into his lungs, enjoying the change from his regular Luckies.

"I wish I could share your confidence, Harry."

"Well, you should, Joe. Buddha preaches serenity in the face of that which you cannot control."

Joe finally laughed.

"That's good to know, Harry, but my guy got nailed to a goddamned cross."

SEDITION

Northern Apennines Campaign
Florence, Italy
39 Months & 2 Weeks After Pearl Harbor

The city prosecutor of Florence kept an imposing office in the Palazzo Vecchio, the ancient municipal building that loomed majestically over the city square. 442 had bivouacked in Florence as the Allied armies staged for the assault on the Gothic Line just to the north, and Major Kimura had appropriated the room to hear evidence preliminary to recommending to the commanding general that Joe be tried for murder.

The prosecutor's desk was at least a century old, mahogany intricately carved at its edges and burnished to a high gloss. The morning sun streaming through the open windows nearly reflected the major's face off the surface of the desk. To his right sat a white lieutenant Joe had never seen before with a pad and pen in hand. The major and his assistant wore ties, the only men in the room in Class As instead of fatigues. The prosecutor had helpfully left a solid ivory Pineider fountain pen in his desk, and Major Kimura now held it delicately between his thumb and forefinger like a conductor's baton as he motioned at the men gathered in the room before him.

"Lieutenant Hanley, are you ready to represent the offender?"

Lieutenant Hanley and Joe were seated in two wooden chairs to the major's left. Sparky, deputed by Lieutenant Hanley to assist in the defense, sat in another chair just next to Joe. At the word "offender," Lieutenant Hanley stood, frowning uncertainly.

"Uh… he's not an offender, sir. He hasn't been convicted yet."

Major Kimura's wintry smile disappeared. He narrowed his eyes.

"Very well, Lieutenant. Are you ready to represent the…"

Major Kimura was searching for a word to convey his disdain without crossing the line.

"The prisoner," he finally managed.

Lieutenant Hanley just stood there without a sound for a moment.

"He's not a prisoner, either, sir. He's still fulfilling his NCO duties."

The major's face began to register his growing recognition that this process might not conform to script.

"I'm ready to represent Staff Sergeant Horiuchi, sir," Hanley said finally.

Joe and Sparky exchanged glances.

The major noticed. "Order in the court."

Joe and Sparky were behind Lieutenant Hanley, who looked from side to side in some confusion.

"Yes, sir," Hanley said.

Apparently satisfied, Major Kimura resumed his best imitation of a command voice.

"The prosecution calls its first witness."

At this, the office door opened and in walked Barney, looking like he'd just run over Joe's dog. Major Kimura turned to the lieutenant doing the scribbling.

"You may administer the oath to Private Hakushu."

The lieutenant produced a bible as Barney turned to face the entire room.

"Place your right hand on the bible and repeat after me: 'I swear...'"

Barney looked down at the book for several seconds.

"I don't know what this is, sir. It says *La Sacra Bibbia*."

At this, Major Kimura exhaled loudly in exasperation.

"It's a bible."

Barney tried not to look at his friends. "I don't know what it is. It's not in English." After a moment, he added, "Sir."

Major Kimura flushed.

"You know it's a bible, private. Now swear on it."

Barney looked straight ahead, shaking his head. He spoke more slowly now. "I can't swear on a book if I don't know what it is."

The major appeared to have trouble remaining seated.

"It's 'sir' and it's got a cross on the cover."

Barney looked back at the book and actually appeared to shrug. His voice had no inflection now.

"I can't swear on a Christian book. I'm Buddhist."

Major Kimura actually stood halfway out of his chair, saying, "Don't play games."

Lieutenant Hanley stood up. "Objection. Badgering the witness."

Joe turned admiringly to his representative.

Lieutenant Hanley didn't bother to whisper. "I saw someone say it in a movie."

Sparky made the mistake of laughing before he could stop himself.

The major clenched both hands and the blood seemed to leave his knuckles and fill his face. He was completely out of his chair. His voice was a squeal.

"Just swear on goddamned Buddha, then."

At this, Barney turned slowly to the major. His voice was a couple of octaves lower.

"He may not be your god, sir, but he's mine."

Major Kimura dropped the ivory pen and leaned on his desktop with both hands. He looked from one side to the other, struggling to catch his breath and speaking to everyone now.

"Enough bullshit. This is all a formality. Horiuchi already told his priest he did it."

The room went very still. Major Kimura's whole person seemed to subside with the wish that he had stopped earlier.

Lieutenant Hanley looked at Joe inquiringly.

"He listened in on my confession with the visiting chaplain," Joe whispered.

Lieutenant Hanley stood again. He was not a particularly good Catholic, but he was at this moment an angry one. He actually pointed at his superior officer.

"You eavesdropped on a sacrament of the Holy Roman Church?"

"This is fucking mutiny," Major Kimura screamed. "I'll have every one of you sons of bitches on charges!"

Lieutenant Hanley, ordinarily a paragon of military courtesy, put his hands on his hips. "Go right ahead, cocksucker."

Joe, Sparky and Barney just stared in amazement. The scribbling lieutenant bent low over his pad, his hand moving furiously.

Lieutenant Hanley's face began to register regret. Major Kimura slowly straightened. The look on his face made everyone happy he wasn't carrying a sidearm. He addressed the scribbler without looking at him or using his name.

"Go get the MPs."

The lieutenant stopped scribbling and looked up for the first time, turning uncertainly from one face to the other as he took in the room.

Major Kimura's eyes settled on the man as he hesitated. His pristine digits balled into dainty fists. "Now."

The hapless note taker looked on open-mouthed.

The major spun to face him, spitting as he spoke. "You, goddamn it! Get off your stupid ass and go for the MPs."

The pen hovered motionless over the man's notes as he just continued to gawp.

"Everyone is this room is being charged with mutiny," Major Kimura sprayed at the man.

Finally, the field expedient stenographer spoke.

"Me too, sir?"

Major Kimura licked the spittle from his lips and considered for a moment.

"No, not you, Lieutenant."

He was recovering his breath as he looked around the room. The major had recovered the ivory pen and was holding it like a dagger. He turned to Lieutenant Hanley.

"You're going down with the rest of them, smartass. This is a military court, not a fucking frat party."

Lieutenant Hanley said nothing. The note taker still had not moved and the major spun on him now. He was breathing again, but his words still came out in a sibilant wheeze.

"Lieutenant... what the fuck is your name anyway?"

The note taker stood.

"Hayes, James, sir."

Major Kimura shook his head tightly.

"Well, Lieutenant Hayes, you're being charged with insubordination unless your ass is out that door in two seconds."

Lieutenant Hayes looked around the room as if seeking guidance from one of the others, but still did not move.

Major Kimura's face grew even redder and he seemed to be searching for more words when Joe spoke.

"I shot him," Joe said, pushing back from the table before him and squaring his shoulders against the back of his chair. "What are you going to do, sir, arrest the whole unit?"

Major Kimura went absolutely still.

"The kraut needed shooting, so I shot him," Joe added.

Major Kimura's face began to transform. He exhaled slowly as his color began to subside.

"I don't think you're supposed to talk, Joe," Lieutenant Hanley said uncertainly.

Joe shook his head. "I'm not going to hide from it."

Major Kimura was a different man now. His face had taken the aspect of a kid who's discovered a Flexible Flyer beneath the Christmas tree when he expected socks.

"You're my witness, Haynes," he said.

"It's Hayes, sir."

"Hayes then. Write that down. 'The kraut needed killing, so I killed him.'"

"I think he said 'shooting,' sir. 'The kraut needed shooting, so I shot him.'"

"That's what I said, goddammit. Write!"

The scribe sat back down and bent dutifully to his notepad. Major Kimura put his hands on his hips and turned to the other men. He'd regained his breath and spoke more easily now.

"This hearing is concluded. Staff Sergeant Horiuchi's confession has established that he did the crime."

He spoke with his chin now, looking down his nose at the men before him, which was not easy since they were all taller.

The men stood and began to file out. Joe was the last. As he walked through the door, he heard, "Horiuchi. You'll be notified once the general has convened the general court."

VELVEETA

She held you with her eyes—dark, depthless pools that said she understood why she was noticed. She was sleek, her curves colliding gently with one another as she tossed her head slightly, luxuriating in the light breeze. Men felt her power and she knew it.

Joe turned to the man next to him. "Why do they call her Velveeta?"

British Army Lieutenant Harold St. Claire had been seconded to the SAS from the Coldstream Guards.

"All of Italy is starving, Joe. She loves that waxy yellow cheese facsimile in your rations."

Lieutenant St. Clair, "Sinclair" or simply "Bunny" to his friends, smiled. He may have known Joe's name, but he called all the Americans "Joe" unless they were operating.

Whatever the yellow cheese facsimile was made of, Joe decided it hadn't hurt her perfect ass, a monument to its intended function. He looked on in fascination as Velveeta walked up and nuzzled the Englishman's cheek with her nose. *It had to be the accent,* he told himself.

Bunny kissed her lightly on the nose and turned to Joe.

"Hand me her feed bag, would you, old boy?"

Joe tried to help Bunny strap the bag behind the mule's ears, but Velveeta pushed her nose between them and began to chew noisily the oats within.

Mules were some of the most important campaigners in the Italian mountains. Sure-footed and incredibly strong, they carried mountainous loads for those to whom they listened. Velveeta and the rest of her mule train listened to Bunny.

He looked like Lesley Howard out for grouse.

Everyone knew the star from *Gone with the Wind*. His death in 1943 at the hands of a Luftwaffe fighter had sparked rampant rumors of clandestine heroics. Bunny not only looked like him, he also dressed like him in corduroys and a waxed hunting jacket. Joe had never seen insignia of rank or unit.

Bunny had drawn his assignment with the Italian partisans because he'd studied in Italy.

"Learned viniculture at Università di Bologna. The consumption end, anyway."

He'd drawn mules because he'd been an accomplished horseman as a civilian.

"On a horse since I was five. Polo, hunting. Best ways to get out of the house."

Joe imagined a house out of *Wuthering Heights*. He'd never read the book, but Fumi had mentioned it. He still missed her, but his impending courts-martial had crowded her out of his mind. Even this had faded, though, as the unit prepared to assail the Wehrmacht in the saw-toothed peaks above them.

Bunny was battalion liaison with the partisans.

"They're all Communists and loathe everything about us," he'd explained, "but the nicest lot you could meet...unless you're a German."

The partisans had spent their lives on the trails and escarpments where the Germans now waited. Now they harried them by cutting their lines of supply, laying ambushes, and generally requiring their former allies to dedicate significant resources to hunting them. Many of them had worked as conscripted labor building their emplacements. They would guide 442 and conduct diversionary operations to draw German troops away.

Bunny intrigued his new cohort. After hearing that the tall Englishman had a polo string of four mares, Lieutenant Hanley had queried him in language intended to convey familiarity with his world: "How many hands is your best mare?"

"Who knows, dear boy? I just mount the poor girl and make her miserable."

Bunny's jokes were a personal preference. His job, which he did well, was to school the men in working with the partisans and the mules as they traversed the slopes surrounding Florence and studied the approaches to the German positions above. This they had done, but he believed in downtime as an opportunity to enhance unit cohesion. He'd already delivered an engaging discourse on the logistics of grass, explaining that Genghis Khan had conquered his empire by choosing his campaign routes according to the available forage for his horses enroute. With three horses per mounted soldier, his campaigns followed the good grass, while the soldiers themselves subsisted on mare's milk.

Humor, however, was his favored means of bringing men together. He explained that he learned this approach as a teenager.

"I rowed at Eton, a secondary school, you call them 'high schools,' outside London."

"Isn't it called a 'public school,' but it's private?" Lieutenant Hanley asked.

"That is absolutely correct, Pat. Please don't ask me to explain. In any event, our coxswain was a diminutive fellow— a Jew, a Rothschild, in fact—who called our rate, steered our boat, and generally kept us out of trouble."

Lieutenant Hanley interrupted. "Your smallest guy was your leader?"

Bunny raised his eyebrows. "Surely you've learned, Pat, that brains and balls have no correlation to size?"

This drew appreciative laughter.

"He became our leader because our designated captain had the charm of one of your Sumo wrestlers," Bunny continued. "Our cox was our company commander without the murderous intent. He led us in training—running, rowing, weights. I noticed that the more he made us laugh, the harder we could train."

Bunny had help keeping his new friends laughing: grappa, the favored inebriant of the Italian peasant. Bunny's partisan friends kept him amply supplied in the clear, colorless liquor that tasted to Joe like the Hawaiian moonshine manufactured by the Paniolos out on Haleakala Ranch. Just the smell of the stuff made Joe tear up. Distilled from the leavings of the wine press instead of mangoes, papaya or sugar cane, grappa came on like kerosene but had a pleasing aftertaste after twenty minutes of steady application.

Grappa was Bunny's chosen medium for his informal "chalk talk." He'd persuaded Lieutenant Hanley to convene one with the mortar platoon during a free evening in the rear on a patch of grass just off the platoon's bivouac on the edge of the city. Rear or line, Bunny never forgot his tactical environment.

"Careful, men. Put down your cups before you light your cigarettes."

The men had arrayed themselves in the heat and light from a conflagration of packing crates and liberated furniture. Typically for soldiers, the conversation always devolved to the same topic: women. Joe simply could not match their liaison's sophistication.

"Remember, men, that the best way to a woman's heart is simply to convince her that you value her as a person. American women seem to be particularly devoted to this delusion."

Despite himself, Joe could not reconcile this approach with Fumi. Instead, he wondered if he should have just told her that he loved being around her?

Bunny was more practical.

"The easiest way to do this is just to listen to her. Trust me men, it's worth the pain."

Bunny drew impassively on his cigarette until the laughter had died down.

"You don't need to be clever. You barely need to be awake. Just keep nodding your head and look concerned—unless she's trying to be funny. Then you laugh, but not too hard or she might think you're laughing at her."

Bunny had his audience fully in his thrall at this point, but Joe was starting to feel just a little displaced. He really enjoyed listening to Bunny and hung on his every word, but this was his platoon, and he enjoyed the respect and regard of his guys. He didn't think a foreigner, bosom ally or not, should hold such sway.

Joe wanted to take the stage, but he didn't want to be rude.

Bunny was pouring more grappa into his cup and smiling with the laughter. The whole point of these gatherings was to get the guys laughing. Soldiers that laugh with each other, fight for each other.

"No need to thank me, men, for the ninety second primer on the fair sex from this soldier of His Britannic Majesty. You colonists appear to be a capable lot. Perhaps one of you could gift the rest of us with your wisdom?"

Without thinking, Joe was on his feet and stepping into the firelight. The grappa had evaporated any reticence, and he barely noticed the radiating heat on his face. He stood there for a moment before he realized he hadn't really thought of anything to say. He put his hands on his hips and surveyed the faces ranged around him in the firelight.

"Thank you, sir, for that learned disquisition."

He figured big words would buy him a little time. His mind raced furiously, and he was trying hard not to sway on his feet. Suddenly, a memory dropped providentially into his besotted brain. He couldn't remember where it came from—maybe a movie.

The laughter had died as his friends wondered how he would extract himself from his folly.

"Bruddahs, you all know me as a man well familiar with the wahini of the species."

They didn't because he wasn't, but he had found his rhythm now.

"Now men, because we're brothers in arms, I feel compelled to share with you my most foolproof tactic in the oldest battle known to man."

The assemblage fell into a silence equal parts amusement and curiosity. Fumi was forgotten now, carried off by the force of Joe's drama. He continued without remembering that his only real engagement in that battle had left him ignominiously defeated.

"Suppose you've spent the required time listening patiently. You've been a perfect gentleman of solicitous nodding, reinforced with dinners, drinks and unverifiable hints of fabulous wealth."

Curiosity began to overtake amusement.

"She's spent God knows how much time with you, so you know you're in the hunt."

No one interrupted.

"Impending bliss is in the air, but the proverbial Rubicon looms."

This was a shameless sop to Bunny. Joe surmised that Sparky was the only other one who knew what the Rubicon was.

"It's time now to impel her into that bed, to 'seal the deal' as the tradesmen so coarsely put it."

Another sop. Joe had never used the term "tradesman."

"Simply utter these words and the magic will follow."

No one stirred.

"'We're only going to have one first time. There's no rush.'"

The hush was palpable. Men took in the transparent competence of the suggestion even as Joe remembered that he himself had failed utterly to pursue Fumi with any competence. He'd never even stopped seriously to consider how to make himself worthy in her eyes—and now he couldn't understand why.

Bunny, however, would not be so easily upstaged.

"Capital advice, Joe, and very regimental of you to share it."

Bunny was about to continue, but Joe didn't care to stand down so easily.

"Bunny, sorry, sir, how do you respond to a woman's complaint about your"—he paused here—'carnal ministrations?'"

Joe had never heard such words actually spoken except by Mr. Alton in class, but he wanted the erudite Englishman to know that he wasn't the only one with a vocabulary. Everyone took his meaning and laughed.

Bunny's smile broadened and he nodded thoughtfully in Joe's direction.

"You know, that's an excellent question, Joe."

Bunny continued to smile as he drained his cup and drew deeply on his cigarette. Then he looked into the middle distance and shook his head.

"You know? I don't think I've ever actually received a complaint about my sexual performance."

A few of the men started to laugh before Bunny looked directly at Joe and, still smiling, said, "Then again, I guess I'd have to be awake to hear one."

LIEUTENANT MASANOBU

Northern Apennine Mountains, Italy
39 Months, 3 Weeks, & 3 Days After Pearl Harbor

Sparky wore brand new lieutenant's bars, but he was not happy. Sparky had been made lieutenant of the mortar platoon, replacing Lieutenant Hanley who'd been promoted to command a company in the 3rd Battalion.

"The colonel has adamantly opposed it to the general, but he still wants to go ahead with it," Sparky told Joe. The regiment was clearing the southern approaches to the westernmost Apennine peaks, and Sparky had found Joe on a switchback. "Kimura's convinced him that Division needs to make an example of you to safeguard the regiment's reputation."

Joe shook his head. "So you're saying they want to lock me up for killing one of these guys if another one of them up there doesn't kill me first."

Sparky nodded. "We've got a regimental officers' call in a few days. I'll speak up for you there, too. I'm sure everyone will back you, except Kimura," he said.

Having heard nothing of the impending trial in some time, Joe had begun to allow himself to hope it would not happen. His newly promoted best friend had just proven him wrong.

"Nothing's going to happen on this side of the range at any rate," Sparky continued. "Division can't spare the officers for a board that would only slow down ops at this point."

The operational tempo had indeed picked up considerably since the regiment had left Florence. The Germans had few static positions below the peaks, but they still had the entire sector registered for artillery. Their spotters put the 88 rounds right on top of the advancing Nisei while German patrols sallied to bloody their flanks.

The Nisei, however, had learned their business. Formations now covered ground with fewer breaks between components. Men moved more quietly. Maneuver elements closed to their objectives more quickly. The mortar platoon, in particular, had become more proficient.

The mules bore much of the credit. Thousands of pounds of rounds, tubes, and baseplates, not to mention food and water, had migrated from the backs of the soldiers to the backs of the mules. So unburdened, the mortarmen could practically skip up the mountain trails. Bunny and his partisans kept the mules moving with sugar lumps and, for the lead mule, Velveeta cheese.

The mules could venture only so far, however. Contact inevitably sent them, and their loads, bolting in all directions. Sparky therefore restricted them to the lower staging areas.

"We're leaving the mules here and humping the tubes and five rounds per, upslope for 500 meters."

"What the hell for, Sparky? It's off the line of march."

"Kimura persuaded the old man that we need to cover the valley highway."

"Nothing that isn't ours has moved on that road in over a week. Why bother?"

"I suspect the *Stars and Stripes* photographer down at battalion might be the reason. Smiling mortarmen in a tidy position against a majestic mountain backdrop."

Contested real estate meant returning the loads to the backs of the men.

Regardless of how much he put in his ruck, Joe never disturbed the wakizashi lashed in its scabbard to the side of his most constant wardrobe accessory. He never removed it from its sheath, but it had become an immutable part of his person, like the miraculous medal his mother had given him that never left the chain around his neck, proof against harm moral as well as physical.

"You've been lugging that thing since we left home," Sparky said, indicating Joe's sword. "Aren't you getting tired of it?"

"Doesn't weigh much."

"Kimura's telling everyone you carry it to cut throats."

"Everyone knows Kimura's an asshole."

"The CG doesn't seem to think so," Sparky said.

Joe changed the subject. "Harry says he heard Fumi and her doctor have selected a date."

"You've got to let her go, Joe." Sparky shook his head vigorously. "You were friends, and you might have become more, but you didn't. You're mourning something that wasn't."

Joe nodded. "You're right Sparky, but I can't help it. I hear a song and I see her face."

*   *   *

A quarter of a mile nearly straight up with baseplate and rounds, plus rifle, had left Joe inhaling in convulsive gasps by the time he finally made the designated ridgeline an hour later. The mountain cool had not kept him from sweating through his fatigues. He'd seen that Kansas was pancake flat, and suddenly, a stint in Leavenworth didn't sound so bad.

Around him, his team staggered onto the narrow ridgeback in similar exhaustion. Too winded to speak, Joe motioned the first two to take security positions up and down slope, respectively. They dropped their rucks and headed out without a word. Joe took out his field glasses and started to glass the slopes beneath them. He noted, not without pride, that his team had already started to establish the position without his having to direct them.

Kimo Wakatsu was stacking rounds in a sheltered declivity. Several others were laying baseplates arranged to afford interlocking fire across 360 degrees.

The ridge directly to his east bore a column of mules moving stolidly uphill along a narrow dirt track 400 yards below him. GIs in helmets too large for their frames chivvied them along with switches and hoots they had probably heard in Westerns. A hundred yards above was a figure moving easily, hand over hand from one rock to the next, while another figure followed more slowly behind him. Accent or no, Bunny knew how to soldier. No German upslope of his mules and his men was going to surprise them.

Joe turned to glass the valley far below. A narrow asphalt track ran along the river at its lowest point. Several OD green vehicles trundled unremarkably in a single file almost directly beneath him. He had swept a quarter mile beyond them when he realized he'd seen the *balkankreuz*, crusader cross, denoting them as German.

What the fuck? he thought to himself. *The road is supposed to be clear.*

"Krauts on the highway," he said as he turned to his spotter and handed him the binoculars. "Heading and range."

Billy Tanaka was already cutting the wadded propellant as Joe's spotter, Chuichi "Charlie" Chiba, called out the range. Joe spun the knobs at the end of the closest tube to orient for the heading and elevation shouted by Charlie and dropped the first round Billy handed him. A pneumatic cough sent the missile in a high arc that Joe followed to its detonation fifty yards in front of the first vehicle.

The vehicle slewed nearly off the narrow road and then accelerated quickly, seeking to get ahead of the section of roadway registered for the forthcoming rounds. Billy began cutting a fresh wad of propellant as Charlie called out a new heading. In the moments it took Joe to readjust his tube and drop the next round, the valley came alive with the reports of other mortars seeking out the interloper vehicles and .30 caliber gunners volleying fire all around them.

What had moments before been an almost pastoral scene erupted in a shuddering bloom of white flashes and brown-black bursts of dust and smoke. Joe kept dropping rounds, hoping for the lead vehicle, when it disappeared in an orange flash of igniting gasoline. He couldn't be sure if he had hit it, but the rest of the column juddered to an impotent halt behind it as the whole valley saturated the roadway in ordnance. He stopped dropping rounds into his tube and turned away from the scene, confident that no living soul would emerge fit to fight.

His guys were watching him. Joe just nodded his head approvingly as he looked from one to the other.

"I don't know how in the hell those poor bastards ended up down there." He jerked his chin toward the peak behind them. "But our fight is not down there. It's up there."

The guys followed his eyes. Bulking against the sky was the western anchor of the Gothic Line, Mount Folgorito.

INTERSECTING VECTORS

Northern Apennine Mountains, Italy
39 Months, 3 Weeks, & 4 Days After Pearl Harbor

A plain fountain stood at the center of a small square with simple sun-bleached buildings around it. Only the church stood out, freshly painted white with a modest steeple. Joe had moved through hundreds of towns just like it, but this one felt different.

Then he realized why. It was completely still in the late afternoon—no people, no vehicles, no donkeys or dogs. The German formations had moved to higher elevations days earlier, but absolutely everyone and everything else appeared to have left, too. His battalion would laager here before moving back into the line.

Joe's squad was the first element to enter the town. He was looking for a suitable billet for his guys when he heard it: a chicken. Suddenly, he was tasting his mother's chicken and rice soup, always fragrant in the confines of their small home. His mouth started to water. Weeks on nothing but bland C-rations had reduced him to foraging for abandoned German rations. Their canned pork and rice was vastly superior to anything on offer from the Army and, seasoned with shoyu, a surprisingly good stand-in for his mother's *butaniku meshi*, roast pork over rice. Now, though, he could taste that clucking poultry roasted over a quick brushwood fire. He unlimbered his carbine and ruck in the doorway of the nearest structure and started off toward the sound of the hapless bird.

It wasn't far. He could hear it clucking just off the square, wandering behind the nearest buildings. He stepped into an alley between two houses and crossed into the abandoned garden beyond ready to dispatch the bird he could hear squawking and scurrying not yards away, just around the corner of an empty stall.

Joe didn't have a weapon. He'd caught hundreds of chickens as a kid. They were all over the island. Accustomed to being fed, they wouldn't spook if you moved slowly. He assumed benevolent mode and stepped very slowly around the corner of the stall. Before him stood a colonel of Fallschirmjäger in full uniform to include a sidearm on his hip. The man was as tall as Joe, fit, and dressed in the camouflage smock and jump boots issued to German paratroops. His uniform and boots were grimy as was the patrol cap on his head, but the jump wings on his chest were still shiny. He stood straight with his hands on his hips as he looked directly at Joe.

Joe gawped. How could he have left his weapon behind? Hungry or no, control of your weapon was an article of faith in the infantry. In country, it never left your side unless you were meeting your mother at church.

Without a word, the German reached for the sidearm on his hip.

Oh God, thought Joe. *He's going to shoot me.*

Joe moved not a muscle as the German unfastened the clasp of the leather holster. It was a Luger. Joe could see it in the holster as the German began to extract it.

Still not a millimeter of movement from Joe. Instead, horror almost to tears as the man drew the weapon from the holster and Joe waited for the ignominious end to his fourteen months of campaigning.

Joe watched as the man turned the weapon in his hand and extended it, handle first, to him. Joe stared at the gun for a moment before he realized his mouth was open. He closed it and took the proffered pistol.

He'd never held a Luger before. They were renowned for their engineering and workmanship and this one felt surprisingly comfortable in his hand.

The German joined his hands above his head.

Joe's first thought was to look to both sides to see whether anyone had witnessed his embarrassment. They were alone. The man had still not uttered a word. Joe indicated the way downhill to regiment with the gun and the German started to walk in front of Joe.

Joe had never seen a prisoner of this rank before. To his knowledge, no one in the battalion had. Joe was acutely aware that he was not carrying his issue carbine, but he decided against drawing attention to the fact by stopping to pick it up. Instead, he marched the man downslope in the direction of his battalion CP at the opposite edge of the village. Joe wanted to convey command, so he pointed the Luger at his prisoner's back. The German colonel, however, was walking easily, managing somehow to convey more command than Joe even though his hands were on his head.

Joe felt ridiculous drawing on the man's back. He decided simply to carry the Luger at his side as they walked. Joe had never fired a Luger. He could tell just from its feel that it was very well made. He wondered: How sensitive was its trigger? What if his footfall set it off? What if he shot his own foot?

Meanwhile, the first two soldiers he ran into stopped digging their fighting hole at a corner of the town square. Their eyebrows rose and one opened his mouth to speak but decided not to. Joe stopped worrying about his foot.

The late afternoon light in the early spring foothills was beautiful, bright without being hot, and throwing long shadows across the slope beneath Joe. To a man, the soldiers gathered at the other end of the square stopped and stared. A German colonel—at least, a live one—was something no one had seen up close. Joe lifted his chin into the sun and swung easily into step behind his prize. Everyone had the same reaction as he walked the man through the town on the gentle downhill grade to the battalion CP beyond.

"Hooch! What the hell have you been up to?"

Captain Hanley was the first officer Joe ran into at the repurposed garage that was battalion CP. He stood in the door with his hands on his hips, smiling and shaking his head.

"Just bringing him in to the MPs, sir," Joe said, deciding not to explain the circumstances of the capture.

The newly promoted captain kept shaking his head.

"He needs to go to regimental G-2."

The captain stepped out of the doorway to escort the prisoner with Joe but realized that a crowd had gathered as every soldier in line of sight had drawn closer to admire Joe's prisoner.

"You handle this, Hooch," he said to Joe. "Well done."

Joe had never actually been in the regiment's HQ before. Today, it was a commandeered chestnut mill below the town. Joe had never tasted a chestnut, but the scent of the place made him want to. It had never occurred to him that a nut could be roasted, milled into flour and baked into bread, but the flour sacks piled at the covered loading dock told him it could.

"Where's the G-2 shop?" Joe asked the admin sergeant at the door.

The admin sergeant was starting to gesture into the building when another man hove into the doorway behind him. His uniform was clean, in fact, pressed—the sharpest Joe had seen in months. His major's brass dazzled off his collar.

Phil Royster regarded Joe and the German without speaking before stepping out and motioning Joe to follow him.

"We don't salute in a forward area, sir," Joe said.

Major Royster was smiling when he turned around. "Thank you for reminding me, sergeant."

Major Royster's office was the mill overseer's cottage. He sat down behind the overseer's desk off the entrance and motioned the German into one of the chairs before it. Joe was surprised when he indicated Joe should sit, as well. Joe was still holding the Luger, but he stuck it in his belt before sitting down.

The German had not uttered a word since Joe had found him. Now he looked around the room without expression. The sun had almost set, and a lieutenant walked in to light two kerosene lanterns in the corner before turning to the German and addressing him in his own language.

The German straightened his shoulders. "I speak English."

He spoke with an accent, but easily and clearly. Major Royster's eyebrows rose very slightly, but he settled more easily into his chair as he recognized that a German intelligence plant would have been unlikely to reveal his command of English.

He turned to the lieutenant. "Charlie, why don't you brew up a fresh pot?"

The lieutenant went into the adjoining kitchen as Major Royster shook a cigarette free from a pack in his desk and leaned across his desk to offer it to the German.

"Who are you?"

"Oberst Peter Hessbach."

Major Royster slid a Zippo across the desk and the German looked at it for a moment before moving uncertainly to retrieve it. Not until Major Royster nodded at him and motioned his assent did the German light up. His rigidly expressionless face softened somewhat as he closed his eyes and took in the smoke to his toes. The whole world seemed to love American cigarettes and this man was no exception.

Major Royster took the lighter back from the German to light a cigarette of his own and crossed his legs as he took his ease in his chair.

"How did you come to surrender?"

Joe felt a moment's alarm. He wondered why he was even still there, but the German saved him.

"I've been fighting the Russians all the way from Minsk. America is the future of the West."

His interrogator nodded. "I endorse your reason, but I didn't ask you why, I asked you how?"

Joe realized he was there to keep the German from lying about the manner of their meeting and started to worry again. When the German didn't answer immediately, Major Royster helped him.

"We've had no major engagement today. Where did you come from?"

At this, the lieutenant walked in from the next room with two mugs of coffee and set them in front of Joe and the German. Joe never grew tired of the smell of coffee and this was fresh and strong and hot.

The German's reserve left him as he took up his cup and took a tentative sip. Germans loved coffee, too. Ethnic German growers in Mexico and Central America had traditionally sent the best of their harvests to Germany, but the war had put paid to coffee, or just about anything, making it into Germany for some time.

The German alternated between sipping his coffee and drawing on his cigarette as he answered.

"I was sent to replace the commander of a brigade that had withdrawn to behind our emplacements."

Major Royster said nothing.

After a moment, the German knit his brows and continued more slowly. "I decline to name my unit."

Major Royster said nothing, deciding not to pursue the question. After a moment, the German fortified himself anew with tobacco and coffee and continued.

"I had joined a motorized column seeking to make the Dolce Pass by taking Route 40 that follows the Fiume Tasso."

Joe realized with a start that the German was describing the valley road he had mortared the day before.

"Our intelligence had few of your units in the area so we took a chance."

The man's English was halting and somewhat stilted, but still excellent.

"One of your mortars bracketed the column and the whole valley opened up on us. The truck I was in went off the road. I escaped through the underbrush and later crossed the river."

Major Royster was bobbing his free foot easily as he listened.

"Did you escape alone?"

"I don't think anyone else survived."

"How did you get up here?"

"I walked all night and laid up today in the town where he found me." He indicated Joe with his chin.

Major Royster nodded. "How did you learn English?"

"I studied it at the University of Freiburg."

Major Royster raised his eyebrows. Joe wondered at the news that someone had actually learned a foreign language by studying it in school.

"Colonel Hessbach," Major Royster said, "the lieutenant will take you to our prisoners' enclosure and see you get a hot meal. We'll speak again tomorrow."

The German stood and inclined his head slightly toward the Major.

"Thank you."

At this, Major Royster took a carton of Camels from his desk drawer and gave a pack to the prisoner. The German's eyes widened as he nodded his thanks again and directed a crisp nod to Joe before following the lieutenant out.

Major Royster threw a second pack to Joe.

"Tell me exactly what happened."

Joe was happy for the cigarettes, but unhappy at their price. He removed one and leaned over the table into the flame the major offered.

"Well, sir, we had just occupied the town. It was entirely empty, so I was reconnoitering the far edge..."

"Who was with you?"

"Uh, I was alone, sir."

The major's expression told Joe that was not enough, but Joe's creative powers had deserted him. He could probably have thought of some tactically sound, or at least plausible, reason for violating SOP by wandering alone and unarmed, but nothing was coming to mind.

"I was trying to catch a chicken, sir."

Major Royster's expression required more.

"They're not usually hard to catch, sir, if you know how."

"You're not bullshitting me, sergeant?" Royster asked with a smile.

Joe shook his head slowly. "There was one nearby, sir. I could hear it."

Major Royster laughed. "You wandered off alone to capture a chicken?"

"Yes, sir."

"Well, I'd say you did a little better. How did you capture him?"

Major Royster's manner had completely disarmed Joe.

"Capture's a strong word, sir. He planned to surrender. I turned a corner, and there he was. He just gave me his gun."

Major Royster laughed again and shook his head.

"This calls for a drink," he said, pulling a bottle of Johnnie Walker Black and two somewhat clean glasses from his desk. He poured two drinks and passed one to Joe. "Here's to home cooking."

Joe raised his glass and took in all of Scotland. Golf was as close as he'd gotten to the place, but the earthy smokiness in his glass conjured up men in kilts and tam o'shanters with daggers in their knee socks.

Joe took a longer slug of what was quickly becoming his favorite drink.

"Do you know why I'm here, sergeant?"

"To question high-value prisoners, sir?"

In fact, the major was relying on a German American lieutenant from Milwaukee who was still fluent in his native language and drilled to numbness with the Wehrmacht TOE, the campaigns of a German unit far from this sector, and every nuance of German military protocol, for that. He had installed this officer uniformed as a lieutenant of panzergrenadiers, his supposed branch, in the dedicated quarters for high value POWs—an abandoned rectory surrounded by two barbed wire fences and four rotating squads of MPs.

The major nodded. "I'm here to collect intelligence on the Gothic Line and the German formations beyond."

Joe was looking at the shoe on the major's bobbing left foot. It was a simple brown Blucher like an issue Class A, but with a depth to the shine that connoted better leather. The major was enjoying his drink and his smoke.

Joe nodded as Phil Royster continued.

"The Army has detached me to an outfit called OSS, Office of Strategic Services."

Joe was relieved that he apparently would not pay for wandering a forward area unarmed. He'd nearly finished his Scotch and the warm glow encouraged his uninvited familiarity.

"Ah, yes. Oh So Special," he said with a knowing smile.

"'Oh So Social' actually, but same difference."

Phil Royster was actually there at the order of his boss, Allen Dulles in Bern, Switzerland, to assist negotiations between representatives of Field Marshal Kesselring and Gero von Schultze-Gaevernitz, a German aristocrat and naturalized American deputed by Dulles to speak for the Americans. Information from accommodating German prisoners, particularly high-ranking officers, could inform the Americans' discussions for the surrender of German forces in the Po Valley—the largest remaining concentration of German troops, and amply provisioned.

Phil had another mission as well. Director of OSS General William "Wild Bill" Donovan encouraged all his officers to be always on the lookout for new talent. The war in the Pacific would be won eventually and Japanese-speaking combat veterans would be useful in bracing the area against the ascendant Red Army of Mao Tse-tung in China.

"What did you do before the war, sergeant?"

"I taught high school English in Honolulu."

Phil refilled Joe's glass.

"Who's your favorite American writer?"

Joe was flush with relief and Scotch. He took a ruminative sip before replying. "Balzac."

He paused very slightly between the syllables and softened the "z." In spite of himself, Phil's smile broadened. General Donovan always said that the ideal OSS officer would be a Ph.D. who could win a bar fight.

"What's your name, sergeant?"

"Horiuchi, Joseph. Joe, sir."

Phil passed him a notepad and a piece of paper.

"Write that down for me with your serial number."

Joe knit his brows very slightly at this, but Phil reassured him.

"You're not in trouble. You've just brought in the most important prisoner this sector has seen."

Joe took care to print carefully, anxious to keep the alcohol from showing on the page. Phil refilled his own glass and leaned back in his chair.

"Why aren't you an officer?"

Joe's face froze and his glass stopped halfway to his mouth. He could feel himself flushing and his eyes dropped involuntarily. He was surprised at how easily he could forget his most pressing problem.

After a moment, he gathered his breath, replaced his glass on the desk, and met the major's eyes.

"I'm pending a general court, sir."

Phil looked like he'd been slapped. "What charge?"

"Murder, sir."

Now Phil replaced his glass too. He dispensed with the rule that you're innocent until proven guilty.

"Who did you kill?"

"A German prisoner."

Phil exhaled unconsciously in relief. Joe surmised he was relieved that there was no Italian woman found naked and dead. Phil took his glass back and reclined again in his chair. "Explain," he said.

Joe tried to focus away the Scotch.

"Our first contact, sir. We took some prisoners," he said. "We thought there'd be three or four. There were twelve. We were four, isolated, and their NCO made me nervous."

Joe had surprised himself with his delivery—clear, uninflected. Then again, he'd never really felt he'd done anything wrong.

Phil canted his head at Joe. "What else?"

"That's it, sir. That's my only charge."

"No. I mean what else happened? Why did one of your guys turn you in?"

"No one turned me in, sir. I think everyone was glad I did it, maybe even the other prisoners."

Phil took a pull from his glass, never taking his eyes from Joe's. "Who reported you then?"

It was Joe's turn to seek sustenance from his glass.

"Well, sir, it seems that the regimental XO overheard me telling a priest about it in confession."

Phil's face wrinkled in distaste. "How did the XO come to listen in?" he asked. "And why were you confessing to shooting the German? Isn't confession for sins? It sounds justified."

"I think it was, sir. The priest had encouraged me to unburden myself, so I told him about it."

Phil didn't respond immediately, and Joe wondered what he was thinking as Phil drew on his cigarette and looked absently at Joe. Phil was scouring his brain for a German speaking priest to offer confession to his high value prisoners. He assumed Gero knew one. Meanwhile, he was looking at a Japanese speaking soldier that confessed a non-sin, single-handedly captured a brigade commander, and made subtly lewd humor about a French playwright. Phil made a mental note to take his charge up with Division Command once they were through the Gothic Line.

The bottle on his desk was still nearly full. He leaned over and topped off Joe's glass before doing the same to his own. The sun had gone down and the evening outside had grown chill. Phil put a couple of logs in the corner woodstove and lit a fuel tablet under them. The flames cast dancing shadows on the wall as he resumed his chair and lit another cigarette. Joe decided a Camel with Scotch was nearly as good as a Camel with coffee. Something in the taste of one just kept sending you to the other.

Joe sat in silence enjoying his drink and his smoke, puzzled about what had just passed between them. Phil sat in silence remembering Earl Warren, now risen to governor of California, declaiming down his nose at J. Edgar Hoover for the removal of the "Japs" from the West Coast.

"Why did you join up, Joe?" he asked.

Joe took a moment to draw on his cigarette before answering.

"It's our war, too, sir."

"What about your guys that volunteered out of the camps? How is it their war?"

Joe hesitated longer.

"I guess we all just want to prove our loyalty."

"To who? To the people that screamed to lock you up for looking different? It's been three years and not a single Japanese has been disloyal."

Joe appreciated the sentiment, so he didn't point out that they weren't Japanese, but rather American.

"What do you owe them?" Phil continued.

Joe had asked himself the question. He'd just never really answered it. "It's not a debt. It's a duty. We owe it to ourselves."

ABASEMENT

Northern Apennine Mountains, Italy
39 Months, 3 Weeks, & 6 Days After Pearl Harbor

"The 92nd has been investing the mountain for six months. Several attempts from the western side, the shallower slope, have failed."

Sparky was briefing his assembled noncoms in the platoon command post downslope of Joe's bivouac.

Joe turned to Rick Higuchi next to him.

"Six months?" he said quietly. "Who's the 92nd?"

Rick leaned into him. "The Negroes. No haoles allowed on this one, brah."

"No one has tried the eastern approach because it's too steep," Sparky continued. "But Mount Folgorito is the key to breaching the Gothic Line. Its coastal rifles control all the roads and rails to the Med north of the Port of Leghorn. It interlocks through roads with the other German strong points along the peaks to its north and east. G2 says all of these are poised to support each other against attack anywhere on the line."

Joe felt the beginnings of a flutter deep in his stomach. He was about to venture an unsolicited joke to Rick when Sparky continued.

"Fifth Army pulled 442 out of France precisely for this mission."

Following the rescue of the Texans, the regiment had passed to the 5th Army at the specific request of its commander, General Mark Clark.

"We're going to breach the line protecting the last major German formation that has refused to surrender."

Hopes of an uneventful prelude to their return home died on the faces of everyone listening. No one interrupted.

"We stage at the eastern base of the mountain tomorrow evening under cover of darkness. 100th Battalion will laager in Cerreto during the day while 3rd laagers in Azzano," Sparky continued.

"The 2nd will stage closer in on the lower slopes to the east just after dark. The 92nd will conduct a diversionary feint on the western side."

The rest of the room was absolutely still as everyone waited for Sparky to deliver the punch line.

"We climb the eastern slope tomorrow night and rendezvous in a pincer formation with the other battalions before EMNT below the summit. We assault through at dawn. India, Lima, and Mike Companies of the 2nd will climb first and have some time to recover before they lead the assault."

Joe had a hollow feeling in his stomach. He'd studied the slope. He would be leading his squad of Mike Company. Ascending in one night would be awful. Ascending with mortar baseplate and rounds would be agony.

Sparky concluded. "Lt. Sinclair and the partisans are taking a squad from 2nd Platoon of Able to set up an ambush on the communicating road to the north of the mountain to block the Germans from reinforcing. Prepare your men."

The assembled NCOs began to file out as Joe sat thinking about the challenge of getting his mortars to the verge of the mountain's crest ahead of the climbing infantrymen so as to provide covering fire when they breached the German perimeter. He was getting out of his chair to leave when Sparky motioned him to stay.

Sparky pulled up a stool as the last soldier filed out. He leaned into Joe, but couldn't maintain eye contact, looking to the floor and clearing his throat every few seconds.

Joe's breath caught for a terrible moment as he wondered whether his folks were alright, whether something had happened to Fumi. Finally, he wondered, with a sense of awful certitude, if Harry had bought it.

"Joe, I'm pulling you out of mortars."

Joe slowly exhaled in a delirium of relief. He realized with surprise Harry's importance to him. He asked himself if Bunny had requested Joe join him with the partisans. Had LT. Hanley asked to have him scout for his company? But Sparky's face told Joe that no one had asked for him.

Sparky was actually wringing his hands, still looking at the floor and muttering so quietly that Joe had trouble hearing him.

"You're being reassigned to HHC."

Joe waited for the rest of the sentence...to Headquarters Company pending reassignment to another mortar platoon that needed his leadership, or to a platoon with too many fresh replacements? But Sparky said nothing for several long seconds. Finally, he cleared his throat again and spoke firmly.

"The CG has decided you're too unreliable for the line."

Joe said nothing, so Sparky continued.

"The pending courts-martial..."

Finally, Joe found his voice.

"What the fuck, Spark?"

Joe had a vision of his guys wandering in the woods under the uncertain direction of a newcomer while he lolled "in the rear with the gear" as part of the Headquarters Company. Suddenly, he was out of breath and hissing at his best friend in a low shriek.

"You fucking let them do this to me?"

Sparky only shook his head. Joe felt he might vomit all over floor between them.

"This is how you treat your friend, motherfucker?"

As he said it, Joe remembered that he was talking to an officer, his commanding officer.

Sparky finally looked up. "You know me better than that, you ungrateful fuck," Sparky said, in a tone Joe had never heard before. "I've defended you to everyone who'd listen."

Joe wanted to apologize, but Sparky didn't give him the chance.

"Life isn't fair. You've made the wrong enemy. Fucking live with it and march on."

Joe wanted the conversation to continue, for Sparky to say something to soften the blow, for Joe to say he was sorry, but Sparky stood and walked out.

Joe sat alone in the shepherd's hut that was the platoon command post and looked at the lengthening afternoon shadows across the mountain scape outside.

What would he say as he collected his gear from his team's bivouac?

What would they say?

He sat in silence, descending the rungs of his misery as he envisioned each soldier's face as he registered the news.

Joe couldn't say how long he'd sat alone in the hut when he finally started to stir from his bench, intent on getting in and out of his team bivouac as quickly as possible. As he started from the bench, however, he remembered the blinding white flash of the detonating mine that blew Ernie in two. Without deciding to, he sat back down as the sights and sounds played unbidden in his head like a nightmarish movie: the awful shriek of the 88s, the terrifying rip of the MG42s and worse, the snap—quiet and unremarkable—of the passing rounds as they nearly found him. The taste of the dirt when a nearby detonation jarred it into his face as he tried to press himself into the earth… Franny staring sightlessly up at him again from his poncho wrapping. Harry Nakano splayed impossibly contorted from the blast of his own round. One of the Bravo Company guys on his flank in the Vosges turning to say something as a round caught his head from behind and expelled his face in an abrupt red flower…

Since arriving in theater, Joe had refused to let himself dwell on the risks he would face. Now, he settled back onto the bench as he played his friends' fates one after another through his mind. He felt like he was crawling into an impossibly warm, dry bed after hours soaking wet and freezing in a dark, windy, winter rain.

As much as he missed each friend and hated each scene, he suddenly realized that none would ever feature him. Headquarters Company would be behind the action, coordinating the maneuver elements that would climb up to and through the German defenders.

He was safe now.

Joe knew it was wrong, that he was dishonoring his dead friends, but he cared at that moment only for his radiating relief at the knowledge that never again would he join an assault element.

DESCENT

Northern Apennine Mountains, Italy
39 Months & 4 Weeks After Pearl Harbor

Headquarters Company was an ancient fieldstone farmhouse with a dull red tile roof. The thrum of the diesel generator just outside underscored all other sound as Joe walked in the next morning with his ruck and his carbine. This last he held almost absently, secure now in the belief that he'd never again have to use it.

It took a moment to adjust to the relative gloom of the interior after the bright morning sun. As he stood in the open doorway blinking, Joe took in the bustle of the room. Maps covered most of the walls. Rosters of men, units, and equipment covered the rest. A bank of field telephones filled one desk in front of an intent sergeant speaking quickly into one. The company commander and his executive officer, the CO and the XO, sat in front of packing crates behind a couple of OD green filing cabinets separating the two officers from everyone else.

Joe nodded to himself as he listened to the clamor of conversations and typewriters. This was their war—paper and talk moving chaotically but somehow coordinating the progress of one hundred mortarmen ranged in support of riflemen from other companies across miles of surrounding terrain. Joe realized he could get used to this; in fact, he already had. This room and others like it would be where he would serve out his war. He could've sung.

"Hooch, you'll help Kanemitsu run the runners."

Second lieutenant Ronnie Takata was another of the few NCOs promoted to officer rank in the field. Joe searched his XO's face for scorn or disappointment, but Ronnie had already turned to someone else.

The sergeant major, Mike Kajima, walked up to him to explain.

"We've got ten guys running supplies and messages to the platoons up front. Kikugawa has them all on this map and indicated by number and color. He makes sure they're carrying what and where they're supposed to. You make sure he has what he needs."

The sergeant major indicated with his chin where Joe could sit while he waited for his absent supervisor. Joe's new foxhole was a pair of stacked packing pallets off to one side of the room. Joe settled himself onto the splintery pine of the pallet and decided it was really quite comfortable. As he sat there waiting to be told what to do, he noticed a new issue of *Stars and Stripes* on the floor. He didn't want to pick it up and start reading in his first thirty seconds on the job, so he tried to read it from where he sat.

The first page above the fold was filled by a photo over a headline in bold: "Family Receives Personal Effects at Heart Mountain Relocation Camp."

The black and white image was somewhat grainy, but clear enough to convey the faces of the people in the shot. An older man with his jaw set looked straight ahead without expression. He wore the brown garrison cap and stiff-necked tunic of a World War I doughboy with a line of campaign ribbons over his left breast. Next to him stood a younger man in an Army uniform bearing lieutenant's bars and the distinctive red, white, blue and green shoulder shield of Merrill's Marauders.

Joe had read about this unit rangering deep behind Japanese lines in Burma. This lieutenant had spent months, probably as a Japanese language translator and interrogator, slogging through the interminable wet heat of the jungle harrying, and eventually defeating, a vastly superior Japanese force. A white Army captain whose face could be seen only in profile was handing a folded flag over a manila envelope to a tiny lady swathed head to toe in a black kimono.

She was extending her hands as she looked up at the captain, small, still and howling silently with her eyes. The caption underneath read,

The parents of SSG Ernest Sakai, 442 RCT, KIA—Sassetta, Italy, July 1944, receive their fallen son's personal effects at Heart Mountain Relocation Camp in the company of their only surviving son, 1LT Michael Sakai, 5307th Composite Unit.

Joe exhaled slowly, afraid suddenly to blink for fear of expelling tears. He was watching Ernie all over again as he pivoted in his own footprints to walk slowly back to the rescue of their friend Tits. Ernie had launched as soon as Tits had screamed "Mine!" Never an instant's hesitation as he painstakingly retraced his steps to his stricken friend and knelt to handle the monster buried in the dirt.

Joe sat there and thought of Sparky, Harry, and the rest of his friends.

Everyone who was left was up on the line ready to jump off at dusk, except him.

For a horrifying second, Joe wondered how Fumi would react to the way he felt now. Joe knew he should feel morose, bitter at his remove from his friends and their imminent risk. He found that he just couldn't. Since getting the word from Sparky, he had left behind the capacity to engage the enemy, to walk into that storm of steel as he had done so many times before.

Comfortable now in the confidence that he would never need to do so again, he could not understand how he'd ever made himself do it in the first place. The serial assault on the senses was more than a reasonable man could bear. Begin with being exhausted and miserable with heat or cold before it even starts. Follow with the noise—shrieking shells, bruising blasts, the high whine of the rounds seeking you out and, worst of all, the screams of the men still alive after the rounds found them. Then the visuals—buildings, vehicles and men atomized under the ordnance in flashes of white, orange and, as to the last, pink. Finally, the smell—burning fuel, burning men, and decomposing flesh, all underscored by the stench of shit from men who'd had theirs torn from them or simply hadn't managed to hold it.

Joe shook his head with the certitude that nothing could make him do it again.

CIVIL AFFAIRS

Rear with the Gear meant better food too.
Lunchtime found Joe idle and hungry at the chow tables set up near a tiny roadside church a hundred yards from HHC. The location was removed from the town down mountain, but a few people were leaving the simple building, probably after attending a noon Mass.

Joe took in the exiting congregants absently as he stood in line for the regiment's meal on offer, creamed chipped beef on toast. Despite its nickname, "Shit on a Shingle" was popular at any time of day and just the smell of the toast and its rich sauce improved Joe's mood.

One congregant caught Joe's eye. A youngish woman stood very slender and straight and wore dungarees and a tweed jacket instead of a long dress. She was not walking downhill to the town like everyone else. Instead, she approached a tent erected by division Civil Affairs across the road from the church.

A handwritten sign outside the tent announced *Assistenza Persone Scomparse*, Missing Persons Assistance—G2's astute ruse for identifying collaborators and Communists. Joe had had only glancing contact with military intelligence, an officer-heavy cadre rich in German and Italian Americans with language fluency.

Joe stepped out of the line to watch her and noticed that she held a small paper, a photograph, in one hand. He watched her enter the tent and decided to wait to eat until she emerged.

He did not have to wait long. Not five minutes had passed before she emerged empty-handed and stood uncertainly outside the tent.

Joe stepped to the front of the line and quickly liberated two trays of the fragrant food, each with a steaming cup of coffee. With a tray in each hand, he walked straight at her with a slight smile, careful not to stumble and drop the trays.

At thirty feet, he could see she'd been crying. She watched him approach without expression, but without moving or averting her eyes, either. Joe noticed her shoes. Scuffed and muddy, they were belted at the ankles, jodhpur boots like Mrs. Alton used to wear when she rode her horse at Lahainaluna.

She took the proffered tray with both hands and said "Thank you" in an accent that nearly sang.

Joe pointed to himself. "Joe. Giuseppe."

A smile, barely visible.

"Fiorella." She thought for a moment, but apparently couldn't think of an English corollary, so she repeated, "Fiorella."

She had dark brown hair with even darker eyes. Joe decided that the music in her voice was even more appealing than the rest of her.

He looked around and gestured with his free hand.

"*Dove?*" The word for "where" being nearly the extent of his Italian.

She motioned with her chin and started to walk downhill on the small road away from the other soldiers. A screen of poplars by the roadside sheltered a low stone wall around a decrepit barn. She sat on the wall with her tray on her lap.

Joe could see she was savoring the smell of the gravy, but she sat perfectly still until he took his own place on the wall at a respectful distance from her.

Finally, she took the steel mess knife and fork primly in her hands and, sitting very straight, proceeded to dismantle her meal. Joe nearly forgot to eat his own food as he watched her. He couldn't help himself. Her movements reminded him of Fumi performing the tea ceremony with her mother.

Having cleaned the tray of every last morsel, she set it to one side on the wall and held the aluminum coffee cup under her chin in both hands for a moment.

She closed her eyes as she took in the coffee's scent, reminding Joe that most Italians hadn't seen real coffee in several years.

She seemed too demure to smoke, but Joe offered her one of his Camels after he'd finished his food and was inexplicably gratified when she took it. A cigarette with coffee was Joe's favorite smoke. He extended his Zippo to her and realized as she drew in that she probably felt the same way.

She looked out over the valley below as she slowly alternated between her coffee and her cigarette. Joe wondered if he could ever tire of looking at her. At this point, their initial exchange had been the extent of their conversation.

When she had finished her cigarette, Joe could see she was flustered by the lack of an ashtray. She crushed the butt against the bottom of her empty coffee cup and looked around for a place to put it. Joe put down his cup and reached over to take the butt from her. The Army had taught him to field strip a spent cigarette to deny the enemy any lingering indicator of your presence. He tore open the paper cylinder and spread the shredded tobacco onto the ground before wadding the paper and putting it in his pocket.

Joe couldn't think of anything to say, and he was happy just sitting next to her, so he just kept looking at her smiling as he finished his own cigarette.

She was looking straight back at him. Finally, without meaning to, Joe arched his eyebrows in a nervous reflex. At this, her chin fell very slightly, and she turned from him and got to her feet. Without a word, she took his hand and led him through the open door of the barn.

The place was musty, with old hay everywhere. Joe could hear mice rustling in the half light. She still held his hand and Joe did not want her to let it go. He could feel her warmth through her hand, and he wanted to draw it to his face and kiss it. Instead, he just gawked as she turned to face him. He was close enough to breathe in the tantalizing mix of tobacco with a very soft hint of perfume.

She looked up at him with a quiet question in her eyes, but Joe still did nothing. After a moment, her expression changed just a little. Her face fell slightly as she continued to look straight at him and reached up to unbutton the top button of her blouse.

Joe knew his friends were on their way to marshal for an ascent into God only knew what at the top of Mt. Folgorito. He knew he was overdue at his new duty station. His new duty station, however, was a room where he was neither wanted nor needed.

She let go of his hand and started to remove her clothes. The vision slowly revealing itself before him left him unable to breathe. She was an alabaster white from the shoulders down, throwing into sharp relief the sunburnt brown of her face and neck. He could see her hip bones and her ribs as he could now the hollows of her cheeks. Fiorella finally stepped out of her pants and dropped them on her jacket and blouse to leave a field expedient boudoir on the hay.

*   *   *

Joe could not have said how long they lay there, but it was nearly dark when she stirred and abruptly got to her feet to dress. She started for the door but stopped when she saw Joe's face and bent to kiss him lightly on the forehead.

Joe watched her walk away. He wanted to stop her or at least to say something.

EQUIPOISE

Northern Apennine Mountains, Italy
39 Months, 4 Weeks, & 12 Hours After Pearl
Harbor

"Where the fuck have you been, Horiuchi?"

Joe was about to lie that he'd been ill, but the first sergeant was too busy to care.

"Grab your gear and muster outside. We're staging on the lower slopes to support the assault elements."

The quartermasters had already stocked the waiting deuce-and-a-halfs with ammunition, water, medicine and replacement radio telephones. Joe climbed into the bed of one and took his place with the others who'd filled all the space not filled with gear.

Why hadn't he gotten her address? Or at least her full name? He swung between giddiness at the recollection of her face and despair as he berated himself for squandering an opportunity to seek her out again.

It was dark now. The trucks rolled without headlights as their drivers used the meager ambient light to follow each other east to the staging area at the base of the mountain. Joe's truck pitched from side to side and jolted hard with every divot in the dirt road's surface. The diesel fumes enveloped everyone behind the cab, catching in the throat and stinging the eyes.

Joe didn't care. He was back in Hawaii with Fiorella. He imagined that he'd learned her address from the guys in Civil Affairs and rescued her from the dirt and want of her war-torn mountain settlement. No more slicing winter winds or freezing spring rains for Fiorella. Instead, the gentle salt breeze carrying plumeria and hibiscus in a sun that seemed never to stop shining on the impossibly blue water against the steep green slopes of the ancient Hawaiian volcanoes that tumble into the sea.

Joe caught himself with a start as he realized that, for the first time since arriving in Europe, he wasn't thinking of Fumi. Fiorella was more than a rebound, he reflected. She was a ricochet. He sat back against the wooden sides of the truck bed and luxuriated in the visions of the life he and Fiorella would share in Hawaii.

She would drop jaws at the Halekulani. Joe pictured her in a light flowered frock under his favorite banyan tree on the patio overlooking Waikiki. He'd be seated next to her—probably in a smart East Coast blazer over one of his many aloha shirts—taking in the admiration and envy of everyone there. He could see her turning heads at the Outrigger Canoe Club, the quiet planter enclave behind a screen of magnolia out on the edge of Diamond Head. Of course, he'd only seen pictures of the place, since Orientals were allowed only as help. He could even see her commanding the crowd at one of the polo matches in Kapiolani Park opposite the Outrigger. Joe had driven past polo matches when he'd taken Kalakaua Avenue out to the east end of the island. The immaculately manicured immense greensward, the horses groomed to shining, the haole women, impossibly distant, languidly taking in the contest from the sidelines...

Best of all, and his breath caught at this, Fiorella's would be the last face he'd see as he closed his eyes to sleep and the first when he opened them, every day.

There had to be a way to find her, he assured himself. The Civil Affairs guys would have noted her name and address. He had only to persuade them to figure out who she was from her first name and the time of her visit.

*   *   *

Headquarters Company had climbed from the dirt track skirting the mountain's eastern base to a small, cleared area hidden in the lee of a ravine on the lower slopes. Even with the mountain in between, Joe and the others could hear the furious fusillade underway on the mountain's opposite side. Mortars, machine guns and small arms maintained a muffled din through the earth and trees separating 442 from the soldiers of the 92nd drawing fire down on themselves from the defenders gathered at the summit. Above it all, the keening wail of the 88s as the German gunners sought to pulverize the mountain's western approach.

Joe stood next to the knot of Headquarters soldiers huddled in hushed discussion of resupply and reinforcement of the troops streaming silently up the slope on either side of them. The grade upslope of Joe was at least sixty degrees in places. The climbing soldiers held to tree branches and each other as they pulled themselves toward the summit without a word. The darkness under the canopy was all but complete and the men followed the luminescent "cats' eyes" taped to the rear of the pathfinders' helmets. These used compasses, maps and red-lensed flashlights to guide their fellows upward.

The soldiers' labored breathing, the scuffle of boots against soil, and the occasional snapping of a tree limb were lost in the undulating growl of explosions and gunfire from the 92nd's diversionary feint. Two soldiers were struggling noticeably. Joe realized why when he caught sight of the stretchers and plasma bottles they lugged between them in the low light.

Joe found himself staring at the summit as exploding mortar rounds backlit its contours against the understory of clouds. Joe remembered that the slope above him was dense with trees and riven with ravines and finger ridges. These were lost in the ink black of the mountain's silhouette, but Joe knew that they multiplied the agony of climbing to altitude under a heavy load.

He wondered how ready Sparky and Harry and Barney and everyone else could be after their hellish ascent. He found himself grateful that he would not see Sparky and Barney, who were already well upslope of him. Mortars would be setting up on the FEBA, Forward Edge Battle Area, before the riflemen assembled to assault through.

He kept waiting to hear an angry whisper asking where he was, but none came. All he heard was the men struggling uphill to either side of where he sat.

Even in the dim red glow of one or two red-tinted flashlights pointed toward the ground, Joe could tell that he was the only man at HHC's staging point without a job. Whispered commands and hand signals were all around him.

He had decided to report to Mike Tanaka, but he couldn't find him. Instead, he found himself standing next to a haole lieutenant he'd never seen before. The lieutenant was chewing an unlit cigar—the smoking lamp was off until further notice. He seemed simply to be waiting for everyone else to kick off.

Joe was about to walk off in search of Mike when he saw the faint glimmer of the branch insignia on the lieutenant's collar in the reflected glow of the dimmed flashlights: Civil Affairs. Joe couldn't help himself.

"Sir, could I trouble you with a question?"

Joe was trying to whisper, but he felt as if the whole regiment had heard him and he suddenly felt stupid. The lieutenant slowly removed the sodden cigar and turned to him. Joe couldn't really see his face in the darkness, but he knew he wasn't smiling.

"What is it, soldier?"

Joe had to say something now and he couldn't think of an exit.

"Sir, a young Italian woman named Fiorella visited your Missing Persons tent today."

The lieutenant returned the cigar to his mouth and shook his head slowly.

"Is this really the time to think about getting laid?"

It sounded to Joe like the guy was almost screaming. He looked around as he leaned in urgently.

"It's not that, sir."

"It's not?"

"No, sir."

"What is it, then?"

Joe wanted to bring the conversation to a quiet and quick close. He wanted to convey serious and inconsequential in one excuse, but his imagination failed him.

"I want to marry her, sir."

Joe hadn't wanted to say that. He hadn't even wanted to think that. He was relieved when the lieutenant laughed.

"Okay, Galahad. She's a widow. Fiorella d'Aglio. Her husband's a surgeon who got sent East with the ARMIR and never came back."

Joe had read about the Italian Army divisions sent off to the Russian Front to support the Germans. The force had been extinguished in the ice and snow of Stalingrad. He resolved that he would somehow secure Fiorella's address from Civil Affairs after the operation.

The lieutenant interrupted his thought. "Aren't you supposed to be doing something?"

"Yes, sir."

Joe moved off to one side of the gathering because no one was asking him to do anything. He propped his ruck and his carbine against a tree trunk, sat on the ground, leaned against his ruck, and waited. In truth, he wasn't even sure that anyone noticed him hunched there.

RECOVERY

Northern Apennine Mountains, Italy
39 Months, 4 Weeks, & 21 Hours After Pearl
Harbor

Joe could not have said how long he'd slept when he blinked himself suddenly awake, but the luminescent dial of his issue Elgin said 0330 Hours. The slopes to either side of him were quiet now, empty of climbing men, but the mountain still reverberated with explosions and gunfire on its other side, although more sporadically than earlier.

"We will stage on the heights just beneath the northeastern edge of the summit…"

What the fuck is Kimura doing here? Even against the gun battle on the other side of the mountain, the man's sibilant hiss was unmistakable.

"Once the mountain has been secured…"

Why isn't he back at Division?

"The photographers will be able to capture the summit against the valley below from there."

Joe was fully awake now. He wanted to laugh out loud. *Is there any part of the man that is not asshole? Am I really listening to my only real enemy in all the world planning a press conference in the teeth of more dead guys with himself as the august speaker?*

Kimura's next words brought Joe up off his ruck.

"Assemble a security detail to go with me, us."

Joe simply was not going to hump this mountain, in the dark, with the Germans still controlling the summit, under command of Kimura.

Joe heard Mike Tanaka say, "Gather a reinforced squad, with a BAR and a crew-fed .30 cal."

Joe had operated both weapons many times, but he did not wish to repeat the experience now with the war all but over, and under the leadership of someone who had none. As quietly as he could, he got to his feet, grabbed his ruck and his carbine, and started to edge downhill into the trees.

Joe didn't know where he was going, except away. As he walked gently into the trees, he wondered how he would explain himself, but he didn't stop. No one had asked him to do anything. No one seemed to miss him. He'd just rejoin HHC tomorrow when the dust had settled. He was entitled to sit this one out.

He wasn't thinking at that moment of Sparky or Harry or Barney. He was thinking of unseen Germans lurking in the darkness between HHC and Kimura's destination, ready to pour fire into the hapless column under the feeble command of a man whose ambition exceeded his judgment.

Joe started to relax a little as he put more distance between himself and his duty station. He was alone in the woods, walking slowly, but easily downhill. He could say he fell asleep. He had, sort of. He'd fallen asleep and gotten disoriented in the dark. So he'd gone to the rear for orders? He'd have to work on that one.

Suddenly, something slammed him in the sternum, knocking the wind out of him and tumbling him backwards onto the ground. He lay there for a moment struggling to recover his wind and gritting his teeth against the terrible ache in his chest.

"Password, you son of a bitch."

Joe felt an instant's terror as he remembered that nobody had told him and he'd never bothered to ask, but he knew the voice above him.

"Shit, sir. Don't shoot! It's me."

The man above him shifted on his feet and exhaled audibly before he spoke.

"What the fuck, Joe? Why don't you know the password?"

"I forgot to ask, sir," Joe said, then added, "Sorry."

Joe thought he could hear Captain Hanley shaking his head as he reached down to help him up with his free hand.

"That's commendable OpSec, Joe."

Joe felt embarrassed by his novice's lapse of operational security until Captain Hanley made things worse.

"What the hell are you doing here? Aren't you supposed to be up with HHC?"

Joe was glad he could not see Captain Hanley's face in the low light, but he could hear it creasing into a frown.

Suddenly, the excuses he'd been composing as he walked sounded pathetic to Joe.

He shifted from one foot to the other and cleared his throat as Captain Hanley waited for his answer. When the silence became unbearably awkward, Joe managed haltingly, "Well, sir, no one had given me anything to do so I was going to higher for orders."

The angry indignation that had lifted Joe from his ruck minutes earlier, that had, in fact, impelled him for the last two days, had evaporated. Joe hadn't felt this kind of ashamed since he'd been caught stealing some of the rice candy his mother had prepared for the lepers at Kalaupapa when he was eight.

Captain Hanley said nothing for a moment. When he finally did speak, he did so very quietly.

"Joe, I don't have time to talk. I'm headed up the hill to replace a lieutenant from Kilo Company who broke his ankle on the way up."

Captain Hanley lowered his voice even further. "You can't do this. Desertion in the face of the enemy is a capital offense."

Joe was tempted to retort that murder was too, but his friend wasn't waiting for his answer.

"Everyone knows you're a good man, Joe. Do this and you're just proving Kimura right."

Joe simply could not dismiss his friend's act of kindness. Captain Hanley could have charged him with desertion on the spot.

He didn't trust himself to say more without quavering, so he muttered, "Thank you, sir" at the ground and turned back up the slope.

*　　*　　*

Joe felt the Headquarters component ahead through the trees before he actually heard them. He was in among them when he saw the dull reflected red of a map spread on the ground and nearly tripped over a man on a stretcher. Joe made out the medic kneeling next to the stretcher as he hung a bag of plasma on an M-1 stood up in the soil on its bayonet. The man on the stretcher was still, but his face shone with sweat in the dull red light and his eyes and mouth were champed tight. Joe wondered to himself how he'd gotten wounded when this element had not made contact.

"He's from Lima Company. He fell 300 feet down the slope and never made a sound," the Medic was muttering to no one in particular. "Broke his femur."

Joe imagined Sparky, Harry, Barney and the rest hauling themselves up limb to limb, rock to rock, in the dark, in silence, to the summit at 3,000 feet.

"There you are, Horiuchi."

A disembodied stage whisper in the dark, but the voice Joe most hated in all the world.

"You'll lead the security detachment."

So much for being unreliable, Joe thought to himself.

"I need a BAR and extra magazines." Joe didn't bother to add "sir," but Kimura, for once, was not standing on ceremony.

"Collect them from the first sergeant and come over and see your route."

Twenty seconds later, Joe had traded his carbine for a BAR and four bandoliers of magazines—forty-five pounds of gear he had not been carrying moments before. He dreaded the ascent that awaited. Unaccountably, he stood a little straighter against the straps of his ruck now.

The map spread on the ground showed the routes of India, Lima, and Mike Companies across the mountain's eastern face, converging at a spot just beneath the summit's rim. HHC's route led athwart their routes across the mountain's lower eastern face to a point above the saddle ridge separating Mount Folgorito from Mount Carchio to the north. Joe could not help but feel relief that HHC's route would not traverse the mountain's defenders. He folded the map into his pants pocket and checked his lensatic compass to assure the needle still swung freely.

The 92nd was still shelling the hilltop and firing small arms from different points on the mountain's lower western face. The German 88s continued to answer, but the whole ruction was no longer as constant, as loud. Joe could make himself heard in a low conversational voice.

"I need two men to each flank," he said, indicating with his blade hand four of the men gathered around him. "Stay ten yards abreast and just in front of the main body."

The main body consisted of Major Kimura, a reporter, a movie cameraman, and several support officers and senior enlisted—all of whom carried only sidearms except for Major Kimura, who now sported a .45 Thompson submachine gun.

"I need you two in trail behind me at ten yards."

At this, he indicated Grant Hirabayashi and another man whom he couldn't make out in the gloom. They nodded in response and gave their crew-served .30 cal a last check.

"RTO with me."

The RTO would stay within ten feet of Joe as he broke the trail—"busted brush" in the infantry—and carried nearly as much weight as Joe. The SCR-300 weighed thirty-eight pounds.

"Hand signals only."

Major Kimura protested. "Horiuchi, we're moving away from contact."

His voice faded as he finished, as if he realized his mistake as he spoke.

"There's no rear out here," Joe said, twirling his right index finger above his head in the signal to form around him.

*   *   *

Joe spent the next three hours navigating unfamiliar terrain, uphill, in the dark, under forty-five pounds of weapon and rounds. Terrain association without daylight was nearly impossible, so he would periodically stop pulling himself from tree to rock to tree to shoot a fresh heading on his compass and try to marry his incomplete impression of the landscape around him with the features portrayed on his map. He would do this by spreading the map on the ground, motioning the RTO over, covering both of them with the poncho from his ruck and illuminating the map under the poncho to avoid revealing their presence.

"We're supposed to cross these two ridgelines. I feel like we've crossed the first," he said to the RTO.

"I think probably, yeah, Sarge."

"Don't agree with me unless you think I'm right."

"I think you're right, Sarge. That felt like the first about 500 mikes back."

"OK. We'll maintain this heading."

"I think we're okay, Sarge. You're following a good line of march. I see you alternating between stepping to the right and to the left every time you hit an obstacle."

Joe appreciated his RTO's infantry skills. Stepping always to your dominant side eventually sent you in a circle.

The night air was cold on the mountain, but the movement still soaked Joe in sweat. He found, though, that the challenge of maintaining his heading exhausted him more than the labor of his march. The RTO had maintained radio silence and Joe was pleasantly surprised that the support branch soldiers in the main body had maintained march silence as well.

Alert to every sight, sound and smell around him, Joe began to see the dimmest hint of the skyline to his east after two hours, their destination ridgeline a flat black against the very deep blue margin above it. At this point, the shooting on the other side of Mount Folgorito was reduced, but still steady, muted through the intervening distance and trees. He could just make out the promontory at the southern edge of the saddle ridge. Freed of the need constantly to confirm his line of march, Joe made for their destination and covered the remaining 750 meters in half an hour.

The surrounding mountains were still in darkness, but a blue-gray dawn was just breaking over their edges. Joe twirled his right index finger over his head and took a knee as the others drew into him.

"Time to stand to."

His security detail started to move to the shrubs at the edges of the bald promontory, but most of the main body didn't move.

"It's EMNT—Early Morning Nautical Twilight. The best light of the day for an attack so we secure our position. We cover our perimeter. Everyone concealed and facing out and watching your section of our perimeter."

The support soldiers started searching for cover in the surrounding underbrush and unholstering their .45s. In the gloaming, Joe noticed for the first time that Kimura was not only carrying a Tommy gun but his web gear was also festooned with every manner of belligerent tool—grenades, magazines, even a fighting knife.

Joe started to direct Major Kimura to a gap in the perimeter when the summit directly above them erupted in sound and light. Mortar blasts were followed quickly by the stutter of the crew-fed machine guns. Flashes of light dazzled against the steel gray sky and glowing tracer rounds arced lazily over the dark landscape. At 1,000 yards, Joe could just hear his friends yelling in the brief lulls between gunnery. Some were yelling "Go for Broke." Some were just yelling.

The mortar blasts were continual, but they seemed to be moving farther away after a few minutes.

"The guys are moving onto the objective," Joe said to the RTO who had crouched next to him under a low bush.

At this point, Joe could hear the answering rip of the German MG-42s—shrill, but fewer in number than the rest of the racket.

"Stay alert. Eyes on your sectors."

Joe didn't really expect anyone to show up, but the unexpected had killed a lot of his friends.

They sat there in silence listening to the shooting and the shouting as the sun breached the peaks to the east and lit the summit in the bright yellow light of the new day. The mortars kept a steady staccato, but Joe realized that the MG-42s were no longer responding. Slowly, the mortar bursts tailed off and Joe could hear the individual reports of the soldiers' rifles and submachine guns, then these, too, started to tail off. Joe wondered how Sparky and the other guys were.

Joe started when his RTO's radiotelephone cackled to life, its ring like a spoon dragged quietly across a tin washboard. The RTO handed him the receiver so Joe could hear the exchange.

"Mike to Samurai Six," the caller said, using the "Samurai" radio handle chosen for the regiment and "Six" denoting its commander. The caller from Mike Company sounded calm, pleased even. "We've neutralized the objective, sir. Lima's mopping up at the far end."

Joe took in the news. Patton's tanks were racing across Germany, capturing more prisoners than they could handle. The Russians were doing the same thing, reportedly with fewer qualms about handling prisoners, from the opposite direction. The sprawling Po Valley on the other side of Mount Folgorito held the largest remaining concentration of combat effective German troops. Their previously impregnable perimeter had just been breached.

"Give me that thing," Major Kimura said, wrenching the receiver from Joe's hand.

Joe could still hear garbled voices discussing the rout of the mountain's defenders through the receiver in Kimura's hand. Major Kimura continued to listen with an expression that approximated his conception of a gunslinger's before handing the receiver back to the RTO. He turned to the reporter and the cameraman.

"We're on, men. Set her up."

So much for standing to, thought Joe.

The light was perfect now. Everything was bright. Even the leaves on a bush were sharp at fifty yards. The cameraman produced a bright new flag on a collapsible pole and a phonograph.

Joe decided he hated Major Kimura more than any German. The summit was likely littered with friends dirty and dead, and this guy had choreographed a theatrical production of himself.

Major Kimura stood with his back to the summit, the flag snapping in the breeze at his side, and did something Joe had never seen him do before. He lit a cigarette. His first draw provoked a coughing fit. Major Kimura thought better of actually trying to smoke it and held it in his hand while the cameraman checked the light and started the phonograph.

Joe had always disliked the regimental song. Someone back at Shelby had shoehorned idiotic lyrics into the Coast Guard Anthem, *Semper Paratus*, and ruined the stirring tune's meter.

We'll fight for you and the red, white and blue…

Fighting for dear old Uncle Sam, Go for Broke. We don't give a damn.

The amazing thing was that the whole regiment had sung it like they meant it.

Now the regiment's recorded voices were baying at full volume. Kimura stood with his cigarette dangling menacingly from his lower lip as he cradled the Tommy gun against his torso crowded with the implements of mayhem, a recruiting poster made flesh. His delicate hands struck a discordant note. Marlene Dietrich's conveyed more purpose.

"Roll 'em," the cameraman said.

Major Kimura turned to the camera and started to indicate the summit behind him with the muzzle of the Tommy gun. Before he spoke, however, a huge boom reverberated up from somewhere beneath them, followed immediately by the rattle of machine guns joined shortly by mortars.

Joe took a quick compass heading to the sound and pulled the map from his ruck to find the location.

"That's Bunny and his guys," he shouted.

A second boom punctuated the staccato of machine guns and mortars. Joe wanted to form everyone up to move downslope and reinforce when the radiotelephone came alive. Bunny was calling for artillery support as the booming cannon began to speak every couple of seconds.

"Muleskinner Six calling Kettle Drum. We need fire on our position. Kraut relief column with armor on the communicating road from Carchio. We are being overrun. I say again. We are being overrun."

Bunny sounded almost languid as he called to be shelled by his own side, but he was screaming over the din of the MG-42s and the 88 mounted on the German tank. These began to displace the percussive reports of Bunny's mortars and the rattle of his machine gunners.

The American artillery began to whistle into the valley. The ridgeline 1,000 yards downslope was a welter of shell bursts, but the distinctive boom of the 88 did not stop. Joe was trying to decide what to do when the RTO pushed the receiver to his ear.

"Who's this?"

Joe recognized the voice of Lima Company's Commander, Captain Hazelett.

"Staff Sergeant Horiuchi, sir, HHC."

"You've got to keep that Kraut column off this summit. I'm sending two platoons with bazookas. Hold until they get there."

"Roger, sir. Over and out."

Joe handed the receiver back to the RTO and pulled his binos from his ruck to see if he could spot the Germans. Before glassing the slope beneath him, he noticed Grant pulling guys to their feet and pushing them to the other side of the ridgeback, putting terrain between them and the oncoming threat.

The flag, the camera, and the phonograph lay in the dirt as the newsmen bounded over the top of the ridge. Joe could see no sign of Bunny or his guys through the binoculars, but the trees downslope were rustling with the progress of the tank beneath them. Joe could see the communicating road beyond the trees.

As he watched, the tank emerged from the trees at around 500 yards and started up the long open slope. The tank's 88 had gone silent, but the tank's machine gunner started to volley fire across the slope beneath Joe. The rounds slammed into the slope with small explosions of soil and scree.

Joe considered the slope and decided it was too steep for the tank to make their ridgeline. He tallied their firepower. With him on the BAR, Grant on the crew-fed .30 cal, someone on Kimura's Tommy gun, and the rest of the security detachment firing in support, he believed they could hold off the following infantry from their cover behind the spine of the ridge, for a little while at least.

Then he noticed that Kimura had not followed the others to their place of cover. Upon hearing the tank's first report, he had dived under a bush. Now he stood in it, thrashing furiously. The bush was shaking violently, and Joe realized the tank's machine gunner was not merely covering the slope with suppressive fire. He was shooting at the man who was shaking the bush like a matador's cape before an angry bull. The rounds were not falling haphazardly. The gunner was too far away to shoot straight at Kimura. He had to loft his rounds and he was over-correcting to left and right as he sought to volley his rounds down onto his target.

The shriek of the gun as the bullets played across the slope brought the leaden stream to life—a *yokai*, a demon bent on murder. Joe started to yell at Kimura to join the others when he realized he couldn't. The bush was a mass of mountain laurel vines that had caught on the weapons hanging from Kimura's web gear. In a calm moment, Kimura could have disentangled himself, but now he only struggled and screamed.

The gunner was finding his range. The fan of falling rounds was growing tighter as it crept up the slope toward Kimura.

Joe was a few feet from safety. He took in the approaching rounds, but all he could really see was Kimura's face. Eyes wide and mouth open, Kimura riveted Joe with a look of abject supplication.

Joe launched toward Kimura. Without breaking stride, he drew his wakizashi from the side of his ruck. He was back at dojo with Ogata-san, but he was no longer the awkward ten-year-old, stumbling miserably through his drills. He flew across the intervening space, his limbs perfectly choreographed as he pivoted in midair to begin his work.

The blade sang in front of him as he planted his right foot and pulled Kimura by the shoulder with his left hand. The vines fell away, and Kimura lunged toward safety away from the approaching hail.

Joe spun perfectly on his right foot and was springing off it to his left just as the gunner found his mark. The first round hit Joe between the shoulder blades. He was already dead when the next three blew him into hamburger.

CARGO

Po Valley Campaign
Seravezza, Italy
40 Months & 3 Weeks After Pearl Harbor

The Army had commandeered a railroad warehouse. 442 and the rest of Fifth Army were sweeping across the Po Valley, collecting prisoners. Field Marshal Kesselring's command and the entire Third Reich would surrender within days, but the men in this warehouse would not see the celebration. Mortuary Affairs had prepared the bodies gathered by Graves Registration and arranged rows of coffins wrapped in flags for transport to the Allied cemetery being built outside Florence.

Each coffin had a small cardboard box of personal effects for shipment to the fallen soldier's family. Most of the coffins bore American flags, but one corner had seven Italian flags and one Union Jack. The cardboard box on this last coffin contained an elephant skin swagger stick, dog tags, and a silver hip flask engraved "H. St. C."

Not far from it was one of the coffins wrapped in an American flag. The box of personal effects on this one carried a barely discernable scent of *L'Heure Bleue*. Inside were a sheathed wakizashi, dog tags, a citation for the Silver Star signed by

"Kimura, K, MAJ, AG," and an unopened letter on heavy powder blue stock. It began:

Dear Joe,

I've broken off my engagement to James.

I miss laughing…

AUTHOR'S NOTE

"[T]he 442nd's actions distinguished them as the most decorated unit for its size and length of service in the history of the US Military."

—The National WWII Museum, New Orleans, September 24, 2020.

Aside from the national figures and the Regimental and Division Commanders, the characters in this book are composites of men who served in the unit. SFC Ernie Sakai did not. SFC Ernest Seichi Sakai was an actual soldier from the Islands who served not with 442, but with the 23rd Infantry, the Americal Division, in the Republic of Viet-Nam. He died at the age of twenty-eight on June 19, 1968, in Quang Nam Province in the same way as his namesake in this book, rescuing a stricken comrade who had tripped a land mine. The real SFC Sakai, however, was not immediately killed by the blast of the mine he sought to defuse. He was medevacked to a field hospital where he succumbed to his wounds after languishing without immediate treatment due to the mistaken belief that he was Vietnamese.

Alexandria, Virginia
December 30, 2023

ABOUT THE AUTHOR

John Kiyonaga is a criminal defense lawyer and former Army officer who practices law in Alexandria, Virginia and lives with his wife on a horse farm in Central Virginia.